Fire and Ice

written by
Paul Godfrey
and
Rachel Borgo

Content Warnings

Pregnancy

Miscarriages

Infidelity

Chapter 1

Kathleen twists the dial on the stove, waiting for those three familiar clicks before the bright blue flame licks the pan. Once the butter is frothy, she cracks two eggs and lets them plop with a satisfying sizzle, careful not to needlessly touch them. Sunny side up with a pinch of flaky sea salt and just a hint of pepper is the way she learned to make them for her husband.

Eyeing the clock, Kathleen covers the pan and traps the heat before she checks on her own breakfast. Sunny side up is too runny in the yolk and too gummy in the whites for her taste. Her eggs boil in a pot of steaming water on the neighboring burner, minutes from perfection.

A soft shuffle of feet precedes a gentle kiss on the back of her neck. *Michael.*

"Good morning, chef," he murmurs, and Kathleen can feel his smile.

"Good morning," she repeats with a chuckle, squirming as his breath tickles her ear.

"Shall I prep the toast?"

She swats his reaching hands. "Sit down. Coffee's in the pot, for better or worse."

"Yes, chef," he grunts, all but saluting.

In the corner of their kitchen sits a small television amongst the clutter of mail, receipts, and recipes. Michael's chair squeaks against the hardwood as he settles in for the morning news with a brimming cup of coffee—black, just like always. Hearing the clink of metal on porcelain, Kathleen smiles as Michael prepares her portion with a heaping spoonful of sugar and a hearty splash of milk.

Just how I like it, she muses.

The morning news rambles in the background as Kathleen plates the food. Two wobbly eggs sit like yellow eyes on Michael's toast, watching her as she peels her hard-boiled eggs. With breakfast now plated, Kathleen joins Michael before the television, dropping a kiss on his lips.

"Mmm. Doctor says I shouldn't have so many sweets before breakfast," Michael says, his solemn frown doing very little to mask the twinkle in his eye.

"Says the man who won't put sugar in his coffee."

He gives the mug hovering before his lips a good sniff. "We need a new machine."

"This week," she adds.

"This week," he agrees, and their eyes drift to the screen before them.

"… and no rain for the rest of the week," the meteorologist says, pointing to a map of central Kansas covered in gradients of red, looking like a severe sunburn. The people of Middle America have grown sick of seeing this very map. The drought extends on all sides of the forgotten little town of Thistle Grove, sapping the color from the grass and leaving the once idyllic destination spot a dullish sort of gray.

The morning news hasn't lost hope though. "A passing storm may grace us next week…"

"Didn't they say that last week?" Michael sighs.

Kathleen is still mourning the garden she planted earlier this spring. "They sure did."

As a commercial begins, Michael leans forward with a huff, grabbing the remote. "Let's see what's happening across the pond, hm?"

It's a tradition Michael has instilled in Kathleen: to care about the UK—not with any earnest investment in its politics or history, but rather with a lazy sort of delight. He has distant family there, and it's been a perfectly lovely vacation spot without breaking the bank.

"—strange morning it has been," the correspondent projects from inside of a fluttering yellow raincoat. Her thick Welsh accent is somehow even heavier than the torrential downpour around her. "I'm on the scene with a witness, who claims to have encountered a creature—"

"No droughts in Wales," Michael grumbles through a bite of his toast.

"Did you hear that? A creature?" Kathleen snags the remote from his hand, notching the volume up by two clicks. The witness speaks in her native tongue, translation subtitles sprinting across the screen to keep up.

"It stood a story tall, no lie," she describes, her harrowed expression framed by wet strands of dark, stringy hair. "I'm not being funny. It was standing there in neighbor May's yard. Its skin was all wrong, green like a vegetable, with horns 'round his head like a ram's! Speaking to her—Neighbor May, that is—it sounded right Welsh. 'It's me,' it kept saying. 'It's me! It's me!' That's about when I ran inside to tell my mum. She's the one that called the police. The officers came to get it sorted away in a van with black windows. Bastard barely fit. I know I sound clean off, but I'm not being funny. It's all true. Mum saw it too."

An older, hunchbacked scarecrow of a woman shuffles through the background, avoiding the camera with a firm slam of her front door.

"She were right next to me," the witness mutters. "It's all true."

Kathleen turns to her husband to see a puzzled weight has settled onto his brow. She mirrors his frown, up until that telltale quirk at the edge of Michael's sparkling blue eyes.

"*It's all true.*"

A burst of relieved laughter lobs between them.

"She's right about one thing. That does sound *clean off.*" His Welsh accent leaves something to be desired, but that only makes Kathleen giggle more.

"What are people on these days? Why make something like that up?"

"Fame, darling," he returns, this time in his best old Hollywood voice. She swears there's a whole peanut gallery behind those eyes, ready to find a humorous spin on any bewildering thing. It's a blessing; between the two of them, someone needs to have a sense of humor. Kathleen's has long since retired—her worries moving in where the jokes skipped town.

Michael plants a kiss on the top of her head, quieting her thoughts for the time being.

"All done?" he asks, gesturing to the table.

"Yes."

He clears their plates, looming over the sink at his six feet and some inches. Kathleen sits for a moment, just to watch his blond hair catch the window's morning rays. *Like a halo.*

This is their morning routine, perhaps the only one they've managed to keep up with in their fifteen years of marriage. They alternate breakfast preparation with dishwashing duties every other day. Sunday is the exception, reserved for brunch at Madame Butterfried's. Just yesterday they were at the town-favorite diner, enjoying triple-stacked pancakes and an endless supply of coffee far silkier than their own.

Kathleen takes one last sip of bitter caffeine and dumps the rest down the drain under her husband's sudsy hands.

"Thank you," she says out of habit, giving him a peck on the cheek before scurrying up the stairs. If they are going to get to the shop on time, she'll have to abandon her ambitious plan to steam her favorite sundress. If it were more humid, the ten-minute walk from here to there would iron out every wrinkle for her. But it's another dry, spring day in Kansas, and with Diana hoarding thermostat controls, Kathleen knows her cable-knit cardigan will only disguise her efforts to look nice. Better to save the sundress for another day.

She's returning her mascara to its rightful spot on the vanity when Michael peeks his head through the door.

"Ready to go?"

"Almost," she says, tucking her hair behind her ears to check for poor blending. Michael smiles, catching sight of the blue jewels nesting just above her jawline.

"Nice earrings."

Kathleen smirks. "Thank you. A real *stud* got them for me."

Her husband barks a laugh, scratching the side of his head. "That's right. *Studs*. I'll never call them the right thing."

"And that's why I'm the one customers talk to."

"My hero," he says without a single ounce of irony. "I'll be downstairs."

Listening to her husband's receding footsteps, Kathleen twists the studs against the soft, malleable skin of her earlobes. Blue was never her color, so it struck her as odd when he presented them to her nearly… *Has it been more than ten years already?*

He explained it over dinner that evening, voice perched on a scoff.

"The internet told me to give you fruit and flowers. For our four-year anniversary. Can you imagine? They'd be gone in a week. So, I thought, I'll get some sapphires—jeweler's blueberries. Do you like them?"

Kathleen smiled, reading her husband's mind. She knew these jewels carried a double meaning after the appointment they'd had, only a week prior.

"It's about the size of a blueberry," the nurse had said with a smile, holding the goopy probe just under Kathleen's navel.

Michael had squeezed her hand, sitting right next to the examination table.

"Baby Blue," he'd whispered.

Kathleen had felt herself flinch before she could even process the words. He'd seen—because he always saw—and had given her that reassuring smile.

You know better than this, she'd wanted to say. *You know better than to hope.*

Miscarriages are expensive, so the anniversary gifts became simpler after the sapphires, but no less profound. For their fifth anniversary, they sold the bassinet and split the cost to buy matching helmets for their bicycles. For years to follow, they acquired gifts and experiences that they could share. They temporarily let go of their dreams of parenthood to reinvest in their little family of two.

At her vanity, more than a decade to the day later, Kathleen looks back on her second miscarriage like she did the one before and the one to follow a short five years later.

Hiraeth.

It's one of the few Welsh words she can still recall from their brief travels. It means a profound longing. Homesickness. Kathleen has a home, of course, and it's one she's eternally grateful for, especially after leading a life where *home* wasn't always a given.

It didn't help that Michael's mother glowered at them from across the table every Christmas Eve, wearing her disapproval like a thick layer of makeup. To this day, Patricia resents Kathleen for depriving them a Wiseman grandchild. She's never said it to her face, but Kathleen can tell.

"So many rooms in this house"—Patricia would sigh—*"and just the two of you to fill them."*

Kathleen makes for the stairs with a huff, slinging her purse over her shoulder and her cardigan under her arm. Whether she likes it or not, she owes the Wisemans. Kathleen never had money until she married Michael. Even then, it wasn't until Patricia and Duke gave them a loan that they could finally afford to jumpstart their lives in Thistle Grove.

I should be grateful, she reminds herself.

Michael is waiting for her at the bottom of the stairs. He rattles the car keys in one hand, the other on the front doorknob. "What do you think? Walk or drive?"

Kathleen doesn't have to mull it over this morning. She has energy to burn.

"Walk."

Chapter 2

"*Wiseman Wares*," Diana says, presenting the words before her like an invisible marquee. "What do you think? 'Wise about what you wear.' See? It works both ways. *Wiseman Wares* or *Wiseman Wears*."

Kathleen chews on the end of her pen before carefully spelling out the latest contender. Her notebook contains dozens of pithy word combinations vying for the crown of new and improved business name. Nestled between Madame Butterfried's and the town's only movie theater, Jenkins' Jewelers has been a staple of Thistle Grove for longer than she's been alive. That being said, its namesake—rest his soul—hasn't been around for a few good years now. She and Michael should have changed the name when they first acquired the business, but nothing ever felt quite right.

Wiseman Wares…

Kathleen mouths the words, peering over Diana's shoulder at the shop door. She tries to imagine them spelled backwards on the window decal, framed by the dark mahogany wood that coats the entire business in a deep and syrupy regalness. She even tries to envision a customer, stopping under the storefront sign, drawn by the phrase.

By the Wiseman name.

She's not sure if she likes it. Diana waits expectantly, one elbow propped on the counter.

"Well?"

"It's on the list," Kathleen offers with a shrug.

"That's it? Exactly how long is this list now?" her friend asks, swiping the notebook from Kathleen's hands. She flips through dozens of pages scribbled in red ink—proof of Kathleen's chronic indecision.

"Diana…"

Her friend only closes her eyes in disbelief, hugging the black moleskin pocket notebook to her heart like a nun cradling the Bible.

"I'm sure the winner is in here somewhere," she says, brown eyes opening with a flash of warm well-meaning. "I could put these all in a spreadsheet, alphabetize them, and then we could have a vote—"

Kathleen holds out her palm. "Thank you, but that won't be necessary. I'll make a decision eventually."

Diana surrenders the book but not the cause. "Is it the Wiseman part? You know Michael would love the sound of *Kathleen's*. Obviously, you don't like that much attention, so maybe we try a mix of your initials? *MK Jewelers* sounds classy as hell. And if people think we're selling Michael Kors jewelry in here, well, that's on them."

Just then, the shop bell dings. Joseph lumbers through the door, the powder-pink box in his hands adding a splash of color to his otherwise gray and black uniform.

"Donuts have landed!" he announces, placing the box on a glass display case for all of two seconds before Diana waves her dust rag at him.

"Ah, ah, ah! Joseph Thompson! You better not be putting those donuts on glass that I just cleaned of fingerprints!"

Joseph shoots Kathleen a wide-eyed look.

"Of course not," he says, carefully lifting the box so as not to leave a mark. A familiar sugary waft reaches Kathleen's nose before he even removes the lid. "Can I interest you two ladies in a little diabetes to fuel your Monday morning?"

A booming voice calls from the back, "Save me a jelly!"

Michael sticks his head out of the office, glasses perched on the tip of his nose. "You know what, I'm craving preserves this morning. I might have to eat all the jelly donuts."

"Don't you dare, Wiseman!"

Michael shuffles up to the counter, a conspiratorial look on his face as Travis trails behind. "Quick, let's squeeze all the jelly out and give Travis the empty shells!"

"You son of a… ," Travis grumbles, playfully shoulder-checking his childhood friend.

With all the Jenkins' Jewelers employees gathered, Kathleen takes the opportunity to jumpstart their Monday morning meeting. It's a pretty standard week of operations, and they can cover it all in the ten minutes before they open shop. Being the second week of the month, it's Diana's turn to open and close alongside Joseph, neither of whom have anything to report besides Diana's claims that intruders of the rodent variety are camping in the back alley.

"It won't be long before they find a way to get inside," Diana insists through a mouthful of strawberry frosting. "And then they're everywhere. We'll be totally infested."

"You need rat poison." Travis grunts. "Just say the word and I can provide up to twelve pounds of it. Got three in my truck right now."

"That's… alarming," Kathleen says, making note of it, more for her friend's sake than with any serious consideration of gutter rat genocide. "Let's see if the situation worsens, and then we can act accordingly."

Kathleen is a good operations manager; that much she knows to be true. Some of her work is a little redundant, but it's all necessary. As usual, she reminds everyone that their staggered lunch schedules are already posted in the binder on Michael's desk.

"Please take a look before we open so you know what to expect for the week."

"Watch me get the last slot again," Travis mutters, flecks of powdered sugar clinging to his mustache even after he takes a gulp of canteen coffee. "Damn schedule keeping me from my tuna fish sandwiches."

Kathleen bites back the impulse to remind him for the thousandth time that it's completely random—the software she uses to scramble the schedule does not hold any grudges against the shop's all-in-one bench jeweler and repair technician.

Instead, she shoves the rest of her donut in her mouth.

"Here you go," Joseph says, offering Kathleen a napkin as she works on the too-big bite.

As Jenkins' Jewelers' most tenured employee, Joseph has long since agreed to Kathleen's way of running a business. She systemized the practices that Mr. Jenkins half-enlisted and, after months of research, created new standards for safety protocols. After a bit of pushback, Joseph quickly realized that Kathleen's way of doing things benefits everyone. Bottom line, it makes his job as the singular point of security in Thistle Grove's precious metals industry that much easier.

"When I'm not up front," Kathleen continues, "I'll be assisting Travis with our monthly loose stone inventory while Michael finishes up the dealings with Thistle Grove High."

"I've finalized two designs for class ring engravings," Michael reports. "Just waiting to hear back how many they're ordering…" His eyes catch on something out front. "It looks like one of our seasoned customers is here to cut off our morning meeting."

He offers an easy smile and waves, and they all turn to see Elizabeth Jones—or Beth, as she prefers—cupping two hands over her eyes to squint through the glass.

"Well, that about does it anyways," Kathleen says. "Joseph, would you let Mrs. Jones inside please?"

"My pleasure."

Their best customer is apologizing before she's even through the door.

"I'm so sorry," she tells Joseph in hushed tones. "It's such a busy day, and you know, I just couldn't put off another cleaning. Hi, Kathleen!" Beth waggles her fingers at Kathleen, stopping to wipe her feet on the mat. "I'm so sorry for dropping in this early on a *Monday*. They should arrest me. Gosh, I must be your first customer. I am, aren't I?"

Kathleen swallows down a laugh as the finest lady in all of Thistle Grove practically grovels at her feet. "Please, it's no trouble. We're happy to help you with whatever you need, Beth. You said that you need a cleaning?"

"Yes." She sighs, lifting a discrete paper bag from her purse. "It's just the usual wear and tear. They aren't shining like they used to, you know?"

"Absolutely. It should only take us an hour or two."

"I just don't think I'll be able to scurry back here in time for a pickup. Would you mind terribly if I came back—oh gosh—maybe next week? There's no rush on my end. Brian and I have a trip planned for next month, and I'd just like everything ready by then. Is that okay?"

"Whatever works for you," Kathleen says, vaguely noticing Michael's voice traveling from the office, softly underscored by a familiar… *techno beat?*

"They having a dance party back there?" Beth jokes. "That reminds me—the prom is only a month away. Can you believe that?"

"Is Nadine excited to go?"

"That's the thing! She insists she's *not* going. I don't get that girl sometimes, I swear."

"There's time in case she changes her mind," Kathleen offers diplomatically, feeling sympathetic to Nadine's stance. "I didn't go to prom."

"Really?" Beth asks, eyes wide. "I find that hard to believe."

"Oh, believe me, I tried to get her to go," Diana chies in out of nowhere, a cup of coffee from the office in her hands. "Kathleen didn't do dances, and she definitely didn't date. She absolutely could have. She looked like— you know, she looked like a young Sarah Paulson."

Beth clasps her hands together, eyes sparkling. "I can see it!"

"What was that music?" Kathleen asks, desperate to change the topic. "We did hear music, right? Beth and I aren't suffering from some kind of mutual psychosis?"

Beth scoffs. "I wouldn't put it past us."

"Michael was showing Travis something on BBC News," Diana says with a shrug. "Loch Ness Monster sighting or some BS."

The news. That's where she'd heard that pulsing theme before.

"Loch Ness Monster? Do people really believe that stuff?" Beth says with a toss of her thick red hair, not a single gray in sight. "As a Scots-Irish, I can attest that my ancestors? Drunk. The whole lot of them. Whatever they think they're seeing is just their own dumb faces reflected in the bottom of a bottle of whiskey."

"I love the UK slander." Diana laughs.

"Oh, it's overrated over there. Brian and I went on a trip once—rained the whole time. Though we could certainly benefit from some of that over here in *Sizzlin' Stove*, couldn't we? Get it? Like Thistle Grove, but *Sizzlin' Stove*? Nadine came up with it. She's got a way with words, that girl."

"Do you know if Nadine is looking for work?" Diana asks.

"Well, gee, I could ask. Are you needing help here at the shop?"

"Oh no, nothing like that." Diana laughs. "Haley is struggling in Lit class. If memory serves, isn't that something Nadine is good at?"

While the two women steer the conversation toward their daughters, Kathleen feels herself sinking inward, retreating. She's a lurker in conversations like these, wondering what to do with her hands, training her smile to reach her eyes. An odd memory emerges from the murk of her mind, and Kathleen recalls a seventh-grade Diana, crying on the walk home from school.

"Mr. Fritz says I can't do England for my paper," Diana said, tears pooling above her round cheeks.

"Why not?" Kathleen asked, hand wound tightly around her best friend's. She stood a head taller than Diana at the time, often thought to be her babysitter

or one of her older sister's friends. *"He didn't like the research proposal?"*

"He said I should do Mexico or Spain because that's where my family is from. But the other kids can do whatever they want. Benny isn't even from England, but he wants it because of that dumb clock," she said between wet hiccups, tears falling freely now. *"I already started cutting out pictures from that* British invasion *edition in my mom's stuff. It's not fair."*

Kathleen squeezed her friend's fingers. *"You're right. It's not fair."*

"And then—Benny said I should just do Wales." Diana sniffled.

"Why Wales?"

"Because he said I am *one."*

Kathleen scrunched her nose. *"He thinks you're Welsh?"*

"No, Katy!" Diana detached from Kathleen and stopped in her tracks, digging her muddy Keds into the gravel. *"He was saying that I'm a* whale*!"*

"You're not a whale. Benny doesn't know what he's talking about," Kathleen stated, outstretching her palm once again. *"Come on, let's get you home."*

A hand sneaks into Kathleen's—the same hand only twenty-some years later. Adult Diana gives Kathleen's fingers a reassuring squeeze behind the counter before letting them go, so quick she might've missed it.

"I've always said that Kathleen would have made a great teacher if she ever pursued it," Diana is saying. "This girl kept my GPA alive, hell or high water."

She must have noticed Kathleen's silence, now making an attempt to include her. Kathleen blinks away the vestiges of her reverie, back in her thirty-seven-year-old body where the topic of conversation has migrated to safer territory.

"It's all gone now." She laughs. "My memory isn't what it used to be."

"Don't I know it." Beth sighs. "Well, I'd better be off. Thanks, girls. I'll pick up on… Good Lord, when did we say? Next week?"

"Next week," Kathleen confirms. "Enjoy your day, Beth. Tell Nadine hi for me!"

The usual lull settles in after the uncharacteristic hubbub of Elizabeth Jones's arrival, so Kathleen leaves Diana up front, following the voices down the hall. She can see through the antique teller window that Travis has Michael cornered in his own office.

"What people don't understand is—oh, hi, Kathleen," Travis interrupts himself, nodding her way before continuing. "What people don't understand is that the function of any governing body is to hide the truth from the people, citing 'mass hysteria' as the reason for a fuckload of red tape and political secrecy."

Michael's computer screen is turned out, video paused on the Welsh woman's glassy stare and her mother in the background, frozen mid-hobble up the steps to what Kathleen presumes to be their modest home.

"And it's your perspective that what this woman saw might be real," Michael says. Kathleen loves him all the more for his earnest investment in the conversation. Travis is the kind of Middle-American with a Gadsden flag bumper sticker on his truck and a fully equipped bunker in his backyard. He lives his whole life from an "in case of emergency" manual, and Michael is an angel for humoring him as often as he does.

"I cannot say for certain that what that woman experienced is *true fact…*" Travis presses one meaty finger into the wood of Michael's desk to emphasize his words. "But I can tell you that we won't hear much more from her, even if it is real. *Especially* if it is real."

Michael nods, seeming to mull it over. Kathleen watches for that signature sparkle to dance across his eyes, but she knows all too well that it won't reveal itself until Travis is out of sight. As if on cue, Travis grumbles about getting back to work, giving Kathleen a gentle pat on the shoulder before he rounds the corner back to his studio.

"Are you spreading mass hysteria at our place of work, Michael Wiseman?" Kathleen teases, taking the seat across from her business partner.

"Undoubtedly," he says. "Travis always has a unique perspective on things."

"Unique," Kathleen repeats under her breath, eyebrows raised.

Michael shrugs. "Keeps it interesting."

"I guess we'll have to tune in tomorrow morning to find out."

Michael smiles, and *there's* that mischievous glint she was waiting for. "Find out what? If monsters are real?"

Kathleen angles an eyebrow. "If we hear from Ms. Monster Sighting again or if she's been 'disappeared' by the powers that be like Travis says."

Michael grins like a little kid. "Like I 'disappeared' the last jelly donut from the box?"

"You didn't…"

But Michael surely did, revealing the powdered pastry in a poorly wrapped napkin. Kathleen reaches for it, but Michael quickly stows it under his arm.

"Who said I'm not saving it for Travis?"

"Are you?"

"Not one bit." He winks, pulling the donut apart in a graceless mess. "Close the door."

With that, Michael hands her half of a mutilated jelly donut, and together, they enjoy the spoils of his treachery between muffled promises to never tell another soul.

Chapter 3

When Kathleen opens her eyes, she knows exactly where she is. Gone are the days when she didn't know where she'd rested her head at night, let alone recognized the same room cast in the next morning's light. Now, she wakes to a familiar scene. Light gray curtains with silver embroidered flowers sway over the windowsill, frame cracked open an inch to welcome in the breeze. The room's white walls are cast with a prescient sort of purple, promising overcast skies.

Could use another layer of paint, Kathleen thinks, not for the first time.

She stretches one hand across Michael's pillow, finding it empty. *It's Tuesday.* Concentrating, she can almost hear him humming in the kitchen below. It isn't until she's at the bottom of the stairs that she can make out the melody.

"'Dear Prudence'?" She yawns.

"Is that what it is?" Michael muses over the stove. "Been stuck in my head all morning."

Kathleen kisses her husband on the shoulder before reaching for the pot of coffee.

More like 'offee, she thinks, tucking the pun away for opportune banter.

Settling in before the television, Kathleen resigns herself to the same news stories, same weather reports, same commercials. It isn't until Michael joins her, breakfast in hand, that she entertains their casual investigation of the paranormal.

"Moment of truth," she says, turning the channel to BBC News.

"—uncertain symptoms," a presenter with dark curls says, hands clasped around a network branded mug. "No matter how peculiar the reports may be, Public Health England is instating a quarantine around Wrexham and the lower Dee Valley. A twenty-four-hour travel ban is in effect while officials learn more about the spread of this confounding condition."

"Are they calling it an epidemic, Nan?" the pinch-faced man to her left asks.

"Words like *epidemic* have been used by the Wrexham community, but no public statement has been issued with any such language. Let's turn to the scene with correspondent Freda Harp, who first began covering the story yesterday morning. Freda?"

A familiar face takes the screen—the reporter from yesterday with her signature raincoat. A prevailing drizzle keeps her hood topside, emphasizing the dark circles under her eyes. Behind her is a billowing wall of plastic sheeting, obscuring her location.

"Thank you, Nan, Nigel. I'm at the scene, standing before the Red Dragon Inn. I, along with the residents of Caia Park, have been quarantined after more reports came to light overnight. According to local authorities, all first responders and witnesses of the green figure have undergone transformations of their own. The cause of the transformations remains unclear; however, townsfolk theorize that it is proximity-based. There is little known while the firsthand accounts of this phenomenon are sealed behind the opaque tarpaulin you see behind me. All we know is that those affected are required to report to local authorities and contain themselves in the now government-commandeered Red Dragon Inn."

While she speaks, the camera pans to a bulletin board. Multiple posts written in the Welsh alphabet bear a symbolic Red Dragon, slowly zooming in on its snarl…

"Oh!" Kathleen gasps as something lands on her leg and *squeezes*, catapulting her attention from across the pond back to Kansas.

"You were bouncing your knee," Michael says, an apology in the stroke of his thumb.

"I'm…" Her focus tears its way back to the screen, now split between Freda and the two presenters.

"And when you say transformations," Nigel grouses, "what exactly does that entail?"

"Well," Freda says. "It's—forgive the reference, but it's something out of an issue of *Monster Mag*. The descriptions offered by the locals resemble the stuff of nightmares."

"It sounds like a Ridley Scott film," Nan says to her fellow presenters' amusement.

The chatter of the BBC staffers dulls as Kathleen squints at the screen. The milky white tarp behind the reporter flutters in the wind, revealing very little. Still, Kathleen finds herself cheering for a sea breeze thousands of miles away. A generous gust pulls the plastic from some scaffolding—*no, the bottom of a stretcher,* she decides. Silhouettes hover bedside, and she thinks she sees a button or perhaps a cufflink. *Just an inch or two more…*

"… and if it's all real," Michael is saying, "then we really have to find a new vacation spot. I could see this drawing some real crowds, though. An elaborate hoax, maybe to market—"

There!

Kathleen's hand shoots forward automatically, finger pointing just left of the reporter's yellow sleeve. As if to spite her, the tarp flaps shut. "Did you *see* that?"

Michael leans in, feeling the pockets of his shirt. "See what? I don't have my glasses…"

"A claw," she says, half-registering how dumb she sounds, half-dauntless in her certainty.

"A claw?"

"There was a stretcher," she insists, "just behind th-the…"

"Plastic?"

"Yes, and there was this scaly *claw* hanging off the edge. I saw it."

Michael nods, taking a long sip of his coffee before he chooses to speak. "What if it's the lizard people, finally revealing themselves?"

"Michael. I'm not a conspiracy theorist."

"I know. I'm sorry. I'm deflecting with humor. It's what I do. I'm a simple creature, and all of this is beyond my limited appreciation for science fiction."

"And what if it isn't fiction?"

"That would be a real treat for Travis."

A few hours later, the town conspiracy theorist picks up Kathleen's argument where she left off, whether she likes it or not.

"The lizard people conspiracy is rooted in anti-Semitism," Travis explains, both hands braced on Michael's desk, "and has no merit in real truth-seeking circles. Kathleen's a smart woman. She doesn't seem the type to feed into that kind of hoopla."

Michael pushes his temporarily located glasses high on his forehead. "Alright, alright, alright. I never said that—"

"Thank you, Travis," Kathleen cuts in, shooting Michael a playfully triumphant look. She tilts the computer monitor to give Diana a better line of sight. Her friend leans in close to stare at the paused video, lips pressed into a definitive line. "I can zoom in if you can't see."

"No, I see it," Diana says, tilting her head one way then the other, trying to see things from Kathleen's perspective. "I just can't tell, Katy. Some people have really skinny fingers."

Kathleen taps on the screen. "You think that's a finger? Why's it so pointy?"

Diana shrugs. "Don't they have mani-pedis in Wales?"

"They've confirmed transformations. 'Transformations in Caia Park have locals—'"

"'—under mandated quarantine.' Yes, I can read, thank you." Diana huffs. "We can't know for sure what any of that even means. It's halfway across the world. This is the first I've ever heard of Caia Park, and I won't be stirred into a panic on its behalf. I'd like to digest my lunch in peace without contemplating the end of reality as we know it. Is that too much to ask?"

Kathleen bites her tongue, offering a neutral expression made easy from years of customer service. "I'm not trying to cause alarm. It's just… it's alarming, you know?"

Just then, the phone rings. Michael reaches around Kathleen to lift the receiver, his free hand landing with a warm weight on her shoulder. After a short exchange, he nods at Travis.

"Delivery in the back," he says. "Help me unload?"

It seems insane that they should continue business as usual, but the two men disappear down the hall, leaving her alone with Diana.

"Screw the schedule," Diana says, tugging at Kathleen's sleeve like a kid. "Come eat lunch with me. We can go next door and get BLTs. And you can tell me what's really on your mind." She emphasizes the last words with gentle but persistent pokes to Kathleen's forearm.

"I just want to talk about this. I've only just started to dig through other reports—not BBC, you know, more local investigative perspectives."

Diana frowns. "Like what?"

"You know, like, like, social media. Unedited videos posted by the public. One shows a woman with feathers all down her arms." She opens her search history, scrolling for the right link. "You have to see the photos of this cocoon…"

"*Cocoon?*" Diana shakes her head so hard her earrings rattle. "No way. That sounds gross. I don't need to see that." She heads for the door, hands splayed at her sides.

"Suit yourself," Kathleen calls after her, proud of her inadvertent job of ridding the room of deadweight skeptics. If she was going to keep tabs on this growing story, she would have to claim the office as her own for the day. "Holler if you need me after your lunch."

"Fine," Diana laments, footsteps receding. Suddenly, her face pops through the old teller window. "You're lucky I love you."

Kathleen smiles. "I love you too."

Once she's alone, Kathleen turns her attention back to her growing list of questions.

In the search bar, she types: *Wrexham monster sightings today proof*

Results populate on the page. It's always chilly in the office, so she pulls her husband's jacket over her shoulders for warmth as she reads.

Small town in Wales quarantined after mysterious outbreak.

Condition reportedly "transforming" occupants of Caia Park, Wrexham.

GIANT GREEN MAN heralds Armageddon in Wales.

Panic spreads as hyper-contagious condition takes United Kingdom by surprise.

As she scrolls through the same headlines and videos she's spent the morning poring over, Kathleen recalls a similar scene at the university library, what feels like a lifetime ago.

"Is anyone sitting here?"

Twenty years young, Kathleen looked up from the computer in the dimly lit lab. Just past the colorful floaters in her eyes stood a blond man, hovering over the neighboring station.

"Um, no." Every computer except hers was clearly available. Who was this guy?

"I'm Michael," he said, like he'd read her mind. He reached out a hand like an intern with something to prove. *"What's your name?"*

"Kathleen," she said, quickly shaking his hand. *"Sit wherever."*

"Your hand is freezing," he said, plopping down in the seat next to her before unpacking a worn crew neck sweater and a familiar textbook from his bag. *"Here, you can wear this if you're cold. What are you writing?"*

" 'The Inefficiency of Trickle-Down Economics When Workers Stay Underpaid.' "

A grin lit up his whole face, seeming to brighten the entire room. *"What a title. I thought I recognized a fellow business major."*

For the next hour and a half, the two discussed the flaws of Reaganomics, turning the conversation to their remarkably similar schedules. Eventually, after some persuading, Kathleen agreed to borrow Michael's sweater. It wasn't for years that Michael admitted to more than recognizing Kathleen; he'd sought her out after nearly an entire semester of watching her chew on her pen in the lecture hall, three rows ahead.

To this day, Kathleen thinks she might not have given him a chance if he tried to distract her from school. Instead, he became a study mate, and then sometimes a tutor, sometimes a pupil—always a source of snacks and laughs. When they fell in love, it felt like they'd already done the damn thing and were now finally letting it control their plans and priorities. It's funny to think how they've changed over the years, how their conversations have moved further and further away from supply and demand and adapted to include, well, everything.

Except for giant green men, a voice in her mind says like a crackling fire.

A valid exception, she argues back, dousing the flame. Michael is an educated person, a level-headed skeptic who asks questions rather than spread misinformation. She can't help but wonder if that's what she's doing. *Is it only gossip?*

Kathleen drops the pen in her mouth to her lap—a habit she apparently hasn't kicked. Diana was right. They can't know what any of it means. This is just like Kathleen finding the latest crisis to fixate on, clinically desperate to put others' problems before her own. If there was a fundraising campaign for the tormented people of

Caia Park, she'd have already budgeted half her weekly salary to the cause.

But all she can do is wait for more information. She refreshes the page.

Small town in Wales quarantined after mysterious outbreak...

The results are identical. A cursory glance at the clock tells her it's past time to drop this silly crusade. Time will tell. The truth will come out or whatever it is that they say.

She refreshes the page—*for the last time*, she promises herself.

As the page fills, Kathleen's eyes snap to a video thumbnail. It's captioned with today's date and the phrase *"anadlydd tân Wrecsam."* It hasn't even been translated yet. Turning the volume down, she clicks on the link and leans in until it commands her entire field of vision.

It's hard to see. A rain-soaked street, brick houses, muddy sneakers? The quality is choppy at best and the audio muffled. It doesn't help that she doesn't speak the language. She's watching a chase of some kind, filmed on a phone, on the run. The runner isn't alone—they're flanked by the patter of other frantic footsteps.

Are they being chased or doing the chasing?

It isn't until they turn a corner that Kathleen understands.

God, she realizes. *It's a child. They're chasing a child.*

A little boy stands at the base of a chain-link fence, attempting to climb away from his pursuers. He couldn't be more than eight years old. Kathleen's heartrate rockets in her chest, a mix of emotions rattling like a can of nails in her head. She can't tear her eyes away, stretching each buffered second for all its worth.

"Dewch gyda ni!" the person holding the phone threatens—*or begs?* Closing in, the little boy's face comes into view. In the dark, his eyes smolder bright orange with red pinpricks for irises. When hands reach for him, his face contorts into a scream…

"What's that?"

Kathleen jolts, pausing the video. She blinks up from the red glow to see Michael standing in the doorway.

"Sounds like a horror movie," he says, eyebrows raised.

She laughs, breathless and short. "It's a video."

His brows inch even higher on his forehead. "Another? What are they saying this time?"

"I don't know. I can't understand them." She shakes her head, eyes avoiding the paused video as she exits the window entirely. "It's fine. I should be working anyway."

"You okay?"

"Of course," she lies. She slides her arms from his jacket, folding it and laying it flat on the seat. "Office is all yours."

He doesn't move from the entrance, blocking her only exit. "You sure you're okay?"

Nothing gets past him. She sighs, hating the shaky stutter of it.

"I'm spooked," she admits. "I just need to distract myself. Can't waste the whole day staring down the apocalypse. There's a shop to run."

Michael smiles, and she envies his calm. "It's not the apocalypse, sweetie." He pulls her in for a hug, and her chin finds a familiar divot in his shoulder. "Want to know what I think?"

"Yes," she murmurs into his shirt.

"I think," he begins, rocking gently, "everyone's sick of that tired old Crown, so BBC is entertaining some of their more bizarre, offshoot beats. Giving local mythology too much screen time. It's all for clicks. Traction." He gives her a squeeze. "Pocket-lining panic. Hm?"

"If you say so."

Michael's lips find the top of her head as her hands clasp behind his back. In her person's arms, Kathleen could almost believe herself a fool in someone's elaborate hoax. More than that, she could almost see past the image burned onto her eyelids.

She could almost pretend that she didn't just watch a child breathe fire.

Chapter 4

Kathleen can't remember the last time she stared at a screen for so long. Maybe it was after her first miscarriage, many nights spent in the trenches of health publications and forums, trying to understand what she did wrong, what she did to deserve this.

This particular rabbit hole is enticing in its own way. It doesn't require much self-interrogation, nor does it seem to affect her or her loved ones in the slightest.

Yet, she thinks. *It hasn't affected us yet.*

Since lunchtime, reports have rolled in like a steady storm. This bizarre, transformation-causing condition has spread in all landlocked directions—north to Glasgow, south to London. Even with the limited knowledge they have on its transmission, experts theorize it's only a matter of time before the epidemic jumps the Irish Sea to Dublin. If it spreads to France, there's no telling where it might go.

When she closes her eyes and sees a map of Europe, Kathleen knows she has to stop. She shuts her laptop and opts for the smaller screen of her phone, piping BBC Radio through her headphones. Stuffing it in a pocket of her robe, she busies her free hands around the house.

When did the fireplace get so filthy?

She scrapes soot from the walls of it, propelling little black clouds into the air. It's a few hours of this before midnight rolls around, ushering in a breakfast broadcast across the pond.

At first, the kitchen is only illuminated by the porch light, hanging just outside of the sink side window. Kathleen switches on the news, huddling in her usual chair to watch the chaos unfold. The presenters talk about seemingly nothing at all, laughing over their morning tea in a strange, vaudevillian game of make-believe.

Behind her, she hears the creak of the stairs.

"Sorry," she calls. "I'll come to bed soon."

He doesn't respond right away, so she turns to make sure she didn't imagine the sound. She catches him mid-yawn, running a hand through his mussed hair.

"Could've sworn you said that three hours ago. Are you going to be up all night?"

"No." She covers a yawn of her own, prompting a snort from him. "What?"

"You've got something all over your face," he says, gently cupping her cheeks in his hands, wiping with his thumbs. "What on earth did you get into?"

"The fireplace," she admits. "I went on a bit of a spree with the scraper."

"Where are your rings?"

"Oh, don't worry." She laughs, pulling them from her pocket and displaying the delicate pearl and solid band in her palm. "Here. Safe."

He plucks them both from her hand before kneeling before her, taking her soot-stained hand in his sleep-warmed ones. "Kathleen Wiseman?"

This joke was funny the first 100 times. "Yes?"

"Will you make me the happiest man in the world," he asks, presenting her engagement ring back to her, "and come to bed already?"

She groans. "I just think that this is bigger than everyone is making it out to be. I'm honestly appalled that no one is covering it here in America. If it spreads to France—"

"If— *If* being the operative word."

"Fine, *when* it spreads to France, it's only a matter of time before it reaches the US."

Michael is uncharacteristically silent, shifting from the floor to sit across from her. He sets her rings on the table to scratch the stubble on his jaw. Guilt hits Kathleen square in the chest. She's gone and killed the comic relief again, the very thing she lacked for half her existence. She folds in on herself, imperceptible to just about anyone except her husband.

In the glow of the television, Michael leans forward to take her hand, sliding both rings back into place. He lifts her knuckles to his lips, planting a warm kiss there.

"I'm listening," he promises.

So Kathleen tells him. With useless, blind-eye journalism buzzing in the background, she tells him that the effects of the condition are unlike anything they've ever seen. Height, weight, and skin tone are only the most basic alterations one can experience. Some have undergone body modifications that are straight out of a fairy tale. Pointed ears. Three-inch talons. Feet hardened into cleft hooves. More teeth than humanly possible and a modified jaw to fit them all.

She tells him that the authorities can't work fast enough to mitigate the spread. Any hope of keeping this epidemic under wraps is moot after firsthand accounts began popping up all over social media. Photographic evidence, personal narratives, video clips—she shares them all.

Michael never interrupts her, not even when she tells him about the cocoons.

"This would be the hardest part to believe in all of this," she says, "if not for the photos."

She opens a photo album on her phone that's utterly littered with screenshots—a preemptive measure in case anything is taken down. A slew of ten or so pictures shows different angles of some kind of organic pod, burst at the seams. Slops of green slime lay in thick puddles where a mattress might have been, evidenced by a metal bed frame laid bare.

"It's hard to know what they look like before they open," she continues, "but the people who've undergone transformations are waking up inside of this thing. They have to break their way out. When they emerge, it's like their beds—mattress, blankets, pillows, everything— were absorbed into, well, they're calling them *cocoons* because, I mean, look at them."

Michael nods, squinting at the photos.

"Do you need your glasses?" she asks, anxious to hear his voice after her twenty-minute rant. It's probably the longest she's ever spoken about anything without stopping herself.

"No," he says, rubbing sleep from one of his eyes. "I can see."

In the silence, an incessant rattle alerts her to her knee, bouncing with enough force to shake the entire table. She tucks the errant limb against her chest. "What do you think?"

His sigh whistles through his nose. "I'm not sure what to think."

No quips, no jokes, no making light. Not even Michael's impenetrable sense of humor can stand up to this phenomenon. That somehow scares Kathleen more than anything else.

"Me either," she says quietly.

"It doesn't…" he starts, choosing his words carefully. "It's hard to believe."

"I would agree with you, but there are photos. It's on the news." She gestures to the television, now hosting some pedestrian weather report. "Not right now, but I think they're avoiding the severity of the situation. Or maybe they're being censored. I don't know."

"What about the people making these posts? How are they able to do that?"

"What do you mean?"

"If a man has allegedly transformed into, I don't know, a giraffe with wings, how is he going onto Facebook and—" He closes his fists to pantomime typing with hooves. "Why aren't these creatures tearing through the countryside like wild beasts, devouring disobedient children?"

"They aren't creatures, Michael," she argues. "They're still people. Only their physical attributes change. Everyone has retained their mental faculties. And as far as I'm aware, there haven't been any giraffes with wings." She can't tell if the sparkle in his eyes is dulled by incredulity or simply the lack of light in the room. "You're not entirely wrong, though. It feels like the stuff of mythology."

"It feels like the stuff of nightmares."

"So you understand why I can't sleep."

His laugh is tight in his throat. "Touché. We ought to try at least."

It takes some convincing, but she agrees to temporarily unplug and join him upstairs. While Michael softly snores, Kathleen scrolls, saving more links, more photos, more testimonies. The last thing she reads before letting her heavy eyelids win the battle is a headline:

Mysterious transformations reach French borders, sparking UN convention.

Kathleen and Michael sleep right through their morning routine, opting to get breakfast sandwiches at Madame Butterfried's. It's uncharacteristically quiet this morning, the overhead TV muted on some kids show. The wait staff clumps into corners, whispering. Tucked away into a booth, they find Joseph contemplating a stack of waffles, doused in syrup. He waves them over.

"They're locking down the borders," he says after their food arrives, "but it might be too late. Mary's sister out in Philly told her that she's already seen one of them, just off the coast."

"I didn't know Mary had family out in Philly," Michael muses. It's a feeble attempt to keep conversation light, talking about Joseph's in-laws instead of the ticking bomb of it all.

"Did her sister say what she saw exactly?"

Joseph shakes his head. He wears two bags under his eyes to match her own. "Nothing specific. But Mary's family has got instincts for this kind of thing. I trust them because—heck—they're always right."

Kathleen knows Joseph's wife more by proxy than by personal experience. Mary is a seamstress, sometimes a piano teacher. She's what Kathleen would call *spiritual.* From tarot card readings to solar rituals, she's not like most of the God-fearing residents of Thistle Grove. Mary has never forced her practices on anyone though. Instead, she offers them for free to interested neighbors who need services that reach beyond their perceptible reality.

Maybe I should reach out…

Kathleen entertains the thought for the first time. It doesn't seem like the right thing to do when she's not made much of an effort to befriend Mary. Kathleen's not in the habit of using folks, and she doesn't want to start now.

Now might be all we have left, the little, anxious voice in her head whispers.

"It's spreading so fast," Kathleen mutters. "It could be here in a matter of days. And then what? We're a-all…?"

"Dreamborn," Joseph says, presenting the invisible term between his two thick hands. "That's what Mary's calling it, at least. 'Cause of the dreams."

Michael grimaces, giving into the discussion. "What dreams?"

"It's a pattern across most transformations," Kathleen explains. "Before they wake up in the cocoon, the affected—or Dreamborn—remember having a strange, vivid dream. But the dreams are different from person to person, so it could just be a coincidence."

Joseph shudders. "The cocoon is nasty. I don't want to know what it feels like to wake up covered in that *Ghostbusters* 'plasm crap. Count me out."

"I don't know if we have a choice," Kathleen says, more to her untouched sandwich than to anyone in particular. She looks up, locking eyes with her friend. "Did Mary say anything about preventing it? Does she know what causes it?"

"She says we'll know when we're next. There's no fighting it."

Michael takes Kathleen's hand under the table. "Surely that's not the case."

Joseph shrugs. "What'd I say? Mary's always right."

Kathleen squeezes her husband's hand. She decides to remember this moment, when all was still normal, sitting at Madame Butterfried's with their employee of the year, every year. She decides they'll have many more breakfasts just like this, whether the dreams, cocoons, and transformations come for them or not.

We have to.

Joseph drops a few bills on the table. "This one's on me."

"Thanks, man. We should head over soon," Michael says. He slides Kathleen's plate an inch closer to her, prompting her to eat something before the day begins in earnest.

"I'll go ahead." Their friend grunts, rolling his shoulders back as he stands. "You two take your time. Something tells me we should savor every moment we've got."

So they do. Michael sips on another cup of joe, and Kathleen finishes her sandwich, one miniscule bite at a time. As she chews, she can't help but wonder if these teeth of hers, these hands—with soot still caked under her fingernails—will turn to fangs and claws. Will her husband's eyes lose their blue brilliance? Will Joseph's broad shoulders sprout wings? What about Travis and Diana? Diana's girls?

Her stomach churns. There's too much unknown. Too much to fear.

"You're thinking so loud," Michael murmurs over the lip of his mug. "We'll know more soon enough. It's all going to be alright. Believe me."

Kathleen nods, picking at the dark crevices of her nail beds. She knows better than to be blindly optimistic, but just for this moment, she'll try to believe Michael like he has so generously believed her.

When the owner comes by to refill their cups personally, Kathleen smiles at her like nothing is wrong. She makes small talk like life as they know it isn't about to turn inside out and mutate into something entirely unrecognizable.

"Thanks, Hilary. Coffee's great, as always," she says, breathing in its fresh aroma, letting it coat her brain with familiarity. She'll savor today, and the next day, and the day after that for as long as the world stays right-side out, unmarred and beautiful.

It's all she can do.

Chapter 5

Apocalypse pending, life at Jenkins' Jewelers carries on, business as usual. Michael has finalized dealings with the school board, and Kathleen has sorted through half of their loose stone inventory. If she were sleeping better, she would have been done by now. Bleary eyes aren't trustworthy, and she doesn't know how many times she's had to start over, counting a batch from the very beginning.

Meanwhile, Diana has dropped all rodent surveillance to focus on her middle child's theatrical endeavors. With the school play opening soon, she spends all of her breaks on her phone, organizing the carpool or arguing with the director about size inclusivity.

"And are the skinny girls playing cows too? Or just my Julia?" Diana prods, phone tucked against her ear as she fusses with the keys to the storage room. "Mm-hmm, that's what I thought. Here's what we're gonna do, Marcie. We'll keep the base costume, nix the spots, and put her in a neutral fleece sweater. Why, then she's nothing but a sweet baby lamb! Okay?"

Diana shoots Kathleen a conspiratorial wink, catching her eavesdropping.

At least I don't have to deal with the Marcies of the world, she thinks. *I hate confrontation.*

Her routine envy simmers into something of a stale resignation. It settles somewhere near gratitude, a quiet place in her soul where blessings are inventoried for later appraisal.

Meanwhile, it's Travis's turn to open up shop with Joseph. From what Kathleen can tell, no conflicts have arisen from the odd pair beyond their usual tensions.

"I swear," Joseph mutters for Kathleen's ears only, "if that man tries to preach to me about the war on drugs one more time, I'm gonna lose it. Like, I know it was a front for some deeply racist BS. Man acts like I don't know what mass incarceration is."

Kathleen frowns. "Do you want me to talk to him?"

He chuckles in return. "Nah, I wouldn't put that on you. That's just our thing, you know? He says his piece, and I let it in one ear…" He gestures—*out the other.*

Kathleen smiles, relieved and a little disappointed in herself. She'll never understand what it's like to be a Black man in a small Midwestern town like Thistle Grove. Maybe if she were less of a universal people pleaser, Joseph wouldn't need to let her off the hook like this. Maybe if she practiced speaking her mind, she wouldn't feel so—

The shop bell rings, and they both snap to attention just as Beth Jones walks through the door. Trailing behind her is Nadine, normally a carbon copy of her mother. Today, however, their shared, defining features are hidden. Beth's strawberry-blonde head is obscured beneath a wide-brimmed sun hat, Nadine's within a tightly cinched hood. A camera bag hangs across her hoodie like some sort of ceremonial sash.

"Well, hello, beautiful people!" her mother singsongs.

"Hi, Beth," Kathleen says with a warm smile. "I love your hat."

"Oh, this old thing?" she says, pulling at the edges of the black straw, casting it lower on her face. "My roots are a mess right now, what with it being so dang busy. Nadine's gone and dyed her hair—get this—*canary yellow*, of all colors."

"Mom," Nadine seethes, almost certainly rolling her eyes from behind her chrome sunglasses. Kathleen can only see some baby hairs peeking out. They certainly are yellow.

"I'm sure it looks fantastic on you, Nadine."

"Thanks," she mutters, uncharacteristically sullen. Nadine has never been one to sulk, so something must be bothering her. Kathleen remembers the emotions of those tumultuous, teenage years like she'd bottled them up only yesterday—like she could pop the lid off and they'd all come raging right back to her.

"Let me get your items for you. I'll be right back."

Beth smiles. "Take your time!"

She returns from the vault with Beth's jewelry in a simple display case. A few strides from the counter, Kathleen clocks a change in Joseph's demeanor. His eyes are wide and staring, practically screaming with significance. Slowly, so as not to draw attention, he lifts his hand, pointing to his ear and nodding toward the pair.

Kathleen quiets her footsteps and listens. She can only make out faint whispers—mother and daughter exchanging words over the counter mirror. Beth leans in close, her hat tilted back as she examines her profile.

"It's confounding… doctors… nothing."

"… the news? Why… to lie?"

Closer now, Kathleen sees something she can hardly believe. Beth's red hair is tucked back behind an ear that climbs too tall at the tip, rosy from being shoved beneath a hat. It takes on a cartoonishly elf-like shape, looking so real for what must certainly be an accessory. Unless…

Joseph wasn't telling her to eavesdrop. *He was telling me to look at Beth's ears.*

Just as Beth's eyes snap up, Kathleen drops her gaze. Their best customer pulls her hat back down, and her daughter shuffles to the side, pushing her sunglasses farther up her nose.

"All my pretties ready?"

Kathleen lifts the velvet display case. "We're all set. Let's see if it's all to your liking."

Beth hardly glances at her belongings. "Shiner than ever. Y'all are the best for a hundred miles in every direction, I swear!"

"Would you like to try anything on before you leave?"

"Oh, no, we've got to be on our way. Nadine's got a game to attend. Someone's got to take those photos, you know…"

Stalling, Kathleen takes her time tucking each necklace, bracelet, and pair of earrings into their complimentary mesh baggies. Did she really see what she thinks she just saw? And if she did, well, what does that mean about Nadine's unusual appearance?

What does that mean for all of us?

Kathleen's best customer service smile reflects across the teen's shiny lenses.

"Well, Diana would kill me if I let you two go without letting her say hello. *Diana!*"

Blind to the stakes, Kathleen's one-woman distraction team emerges from the storage room with her phone tucked against her cheek.

"I've gotta run, Marcie! Duty calls, or at least Katy does," she says with a sardonic eye roll just for Kathleen's benefit. "Buh-bye now."

Beth's shoulders are already angled toward the exit when Diana clears the counter gate and goes in for a hug.

"Hi there, stranger! I heard you and Brian made a trip out east."

Kathleen turns to Joseph, and they lob questions back and forth with only their eyes.

Out east?
How far east?
The coast?
Has it reached us already?

"Lord almighty." Beth sighs, pressing a hand to the top of her head. "It was like Jesus and all his angels were consorting against me, keeping me from my material life. It's humbling really. Brian and I only got back two nights ago. His uncle passed sadly, and the funeral was a layover away. Tragic on all accounts."

"That's awful," Diana consoles. "Please send our love to Brian."

"We're so sorry for your loss," Kathleen says, dizzied. "Where was the funeral?"

"Boston area, and let me tell you, it's not somewhere you want to be right now. Total ghost town. Zero culture. And when you do come across another soul—well, let me just say, there's some strange folk out there."

Kathleen has long since finished packing up Beth's belongings. She slowly folds the lip of the brown paper bag over, key phrases ringing in her head like alarm bells.

Boston. Ghost town. Strange folk.

"Here you are," she hears herself say, offering Beth a discreet paper bag. "Let's get you rung up so you can be on your way."

"Has Nadine ordered her class ring yet?" The question comes from Joseph, who shifts his weight from one foot to the other. "Michael—he was telling me that there's some names missing he would have expected on the list."

Beth closes her eyes, inhaling deep through her nose. "Lord. Another thing forgotten. We'll get that order placed at—"

"You have to do it in the shop at this point," Kathleen cuts in a little too eagerly. *Slow down.* "It's a good thing you dropped in today. Nadine, why don't you come to the office with me and we'll pick out a style you like?"

The teen turns to her mother, who offers a tight smile in return.

"Just be quick about it," Beth says before turning to Diana. "This girl could spend hours agonizing over a new pair of jeans. Light or dark wash, like the wrong choice might activate the nuclear codes. Is Haley like that?"

Kathleen doesn't stick around to hear Diana's response. Lifting the counter gate, she leads Nadine back to the office where Michael looks up from a stack of paperwork.

"Whoa, do we have a celebrity in the house?"

Kathleen gestures stiffly. "Nadine needs to place an order for a class ring."

"Well then, we'd better act quick before the paparazzi swarms us."

Nadine snorts, shoving her hands in her hoodie pocket. "Just because my mom tries too hard for an errand run doesn't mean I have to."

"As is your right," he agrees, suddenly popping a shoeless foot on top of the desk. He wiggles his toes in a brightly patterned sock. "We're business casual here anyways."

"Gross." Nadine laughs, and Kathleen would too if she weren't in the middle of an investigation. She wonders if her attempt to appear effortlessly casual is fooling her husband as well.

"Can you show her the designs?"

"Of course," he says, waving Nadine around to look at the screen. "We've got two styles—honkin' big and tea party appropriate. Gems all cost the same. Some prefer the school colors, and others prefer their birthstone. When's your birthday?"

"October 18th."

"Ah, so do you like opal?"

Nadine shrugs.

"So that's a maybe. Pink tourmaline?"

Nadine shudders.

"So that's a hard no. Opal is a great choice if—"

"What color are your eyes?" Kathleen cuts in. "Sometimes people like to get a stone that matches their eyes."

Michael frowns. "Do they?"

"Sure they do." *Play along, husband.*

"What do I know?" He laughs, angling an eyebrow as if to ask, *What's going on?*

"Hazel," Nadine says suddenly, tugging at her hoodie strings. "But they're always changing. Sometimes they're green, but lately they're like, a lot lighter. Closer to gold."

Nadine isn't as good at lying as her mother. Kathleen could be wrong, but she seems to remember Beth's only child having blue eyes like hers. *Yellow hair, golden eyes… Could this all be symptoms of a transformation? Is it already here in the States?*

Michael taps his chin, none the wiser. "I suppose we should ask your mom if you can get your ring gold-plated… It'll be more expensive."

"I think she'll be fine with it," Nadine says, "but we can ask."

They do, and per Nadine's assumption, Beth is indeed fine with it. In the midst of Kathleen's minefield of thoughts, the Joneses tiptoe with all manner of pleasantries through the final transaction. There's nothing Kathleen can do but watch the door close behind them, the shop bell shuddering in their wake.

Michael leans against the counter, bewildered. "What was up with witness protection?"

"Heck if I know," Diana scoffs. "You couldn't pay me to wear layers like that. In this heat? No, ma'am."

Kathleen can't muster up the words, instead just watching as Joseph steps forward.

"I think," he says, each word heavier than the last, "we should close up for the day."

Michael's eyebrows shoot halfway up his forehead. "Why? Is something going on?"

Joseph is silent, so stares turn to Kathleen.

"Katy?" Diana prompts.

Kathleen finds her voice before it's ready to be found. "It's happening here in Thistle Grove. You should call Eric."

Diana's brows furrow. "What do you mean? Why would I call him?"

"Because we've been exposed, and your girls might be next if you're the one to pick them up."

"What… do you mean?" she asks again, even as her eyes well up with tears. "Exposed?"

Kathleen takes her friend's hand, giving it the gentlest squeeze. "You know what I mean."

"The Dreaming is here, huh?"

Travis's voice precedes him from down the hall. When he reaches Michael, he claps a hand on his friend's shoulder.

Michael shakes his head. "The *what*?"

"Did you see them too?" Kathleen asks. "Beth and her daughter?"

Travis nods. "Saw them parked in the alley while I was out having a smoke. Girl was killing time while her mom was on the phone. You know those shoes my nephew tossed up on the wire a while back? She was taking some photos, and when she lowered the camera—I'll be damned—she, uh—" He clears his throat, scratching at his beard.

"She *what?*" Michael demands.

"She had yellow eyes."

"They're hazel," Michael insists, looking to Kathleen for backup. "She said her eyes were hazel. Right?"

Diana swipes a stray tear from her cheek. "What does any of this mean?"

"It means we'll find out in the morning," Travis says.

Joseph is the first to leave, agreeing to let Kathleen lock up for the night. When Diana finally builds up the nerve to call Eric, she does so huddled in the office with Kathleen, hands still clasped tightly between them. He makes a fuss at first because of course he does. It wasn't in his afternoon plans to pick up the girls from school. It's a sore reminder that he never knew when

Diana's emotions were to be taken seriously, a point of contention between him and Kathleen for years now.

She takes the phone from Diana when her friend's hiccups turn incoherent.

"Eric, this is Kathleen. You need to pick up the girls. Diana has been, um—*exposed* to something, and we don't want to spread it to them. I know it's an inconvenience, but you know she wouldn't be asking if it weren't serious."

"When are you going to stop fighting Diana's battles for her?" he asks.

She bristles. "She would do the same for me."

Eric scoffs on the other end with derision she can't understand. "Alright, Kathleen."

Her heart hammers in her chest long after the call ends. Even so, Kathleen holds Diana for the rest of her cry. It's easy to ignore the flame in her own cheeks while she dries her friend's tear-stained ones.

There's not much else to say as the employees of Jenkins' Jewelers retire before the sun has even brushed the western groves. There's a long night ahead, and Travis's words hang above them like that old pair of sneakers on a telephone wire—useless but something of a comfort anyways.

We'll find out in the morning.

Chapter 6

Kathleen's sleeping bag unfurls with a soft sigh onto the grass.

"When we bought these," Michael says, pulling at the drawstrings of his own, "I figured we'd be in the Rocky Mountains, camping after a long day of trailblazing. Not…"

"Doomsday prepping?"

He smirks. "I was going to say 'in our own backyard,' but that too."

Kathleen smooths the wrinkles of the nylon. "I know it's strange, but every report of the Dreaming mentions the cocoon absorbing surrounding objects. Sheets, blankets, entire mattresses—destroyed. This way, we'll still have a bedroom by the time we're…"

"Different?" Michael offers.

She swallows hard. "Yeah. Different."

The warm weight of Michael's hand comes to rest on the back of her neck. "Why don't we go inside and brush our teeth the Irish way?"

"How's that?"

He flashes her a devilish grin. "With a splash of Jameson."

"I don't know if that's safe."

"I don't think it'll hurt."

Kathleen chews on her lower lip. "I just don't know anything. I don't know what to expect. I don't know if we're even—"

Michael cuts her off with a kiss. "Me either. Let's go to bed and find out."

Inside, they change into clothes they won't miss, just in case the Dreaming claims them too. They brush their teeth side by side, two thousand yards of stares between the both of them. Kathleen wonders if Michael is as terrified as she is and is simply hiding his emotions for her sake, much like she hides hers for Diana's. Which dynamics of theirs will change? Who among them will be unrecognizable after this?

What if I lose him?

She takes longer than he does, smoothing lotion over her freshly washed face and massaging the stubborn wrinkles on her forehead with shaking hands. She already seems so unrecognizable to herself. Brown eyes stare back at her from under her dark brows, the weight of the world hanging from the shadows cast by her lashes. Kathleen tries to memorize her features as they are. She imagines her thin nose replaced with a hideous snout, her full lips curled into a vicious snarl…

Eyeing the scissors on the bathroom counter, she suddenly has the urge to tear them through her hair, chopping off the lengths and letting them fall to the bathroom floor. She wants to make a change of her own volition, not some inevitability that she has no control over.

But Kathleen isn't that brave. Instead, she threads her fingers through the scissors, lifting a lock from behind her ear—as thin as a piece of yarn. She pulls it taut.

With a single snip, the lock lands in a featherlight heap in her palm.

"Can you bring my glasses down?" Michael calls from the bottom of the stairs.

"Okay," she calls back, wrapping the strands around a finger before storing the silky loop in a drawer. Plucking the glasses from the counter, she goes downstairs and into Michael's open arms. Wiggling free, she places the frames on his nose, straightening them on his ears.

"Thank you," he murmurs.

"Don't fall asleep with them on," she warns, not for the first time. She's less concerned that they'll get bent and more certain that they'll get cocooned.

"Yes, ma'am."

It's a beautiful night for sleeping under the stars, only a bit of light pollution marring the view. The grass is bone-dry, the drought working for them as they prepare for a tentless night. With legs tangled in their conjoined sleeping bags, Kathleen can almost pretend this is just another night of romantic spontaneity.

"Thank you"—she sighs—"for being here."

Michael turns to her, and she searches for his eyes in the dark. "Where else would I be?"

"Don't go anywhere," she whispers.

"I won't."

"Don't change too much."

"I won't."

"Don't stop loving me if I change too much."

"You won't—and I would never."

With each demand, Kathleen inched herself closer to her lover, their noses nuzzling. When their lips meet, she can't help her racing thoughts. *Will we be able to kiss like this with snouts, fangs, and any other manner of deformity?*

Clawing her fingers into his hair, Kathleen pulls her husband closer, deepening the kiss. He meets her

urgency with ready hands, wrapping her up in his arms.
With a sigh that starts in one pair of lungs and ends
in the other, the two settle into one another with the
familiarity of practiced lovers. And that is in fact what
they make: *love*, like a promise. Save for the occasional
hushed giggle, the neighbors might only hear the gentle
rustle of nylon among the chirps and croaks of Thistle
Grove's nocturnal residents. Above them, the stars hang
like a winding string of ellipses, punctuating the endless
unknown.

* * *

Kathleen wakes to the smell of smoke. She tries to
wake at least, her eyelids seemingly fused together. Dread
percolates in her gut as the crackle of flames reaches her
ears.

Did we light a bonfire before falling asleep?

In the dark, she reaches a leaden hand toward her
husband, or where he ought to be. Her fingers only meet
grass, dry and disintegrating to the touch. A hot, dry wave
presses against the back of her neck.

"Kathleen!"

Her eyes snap open as she shoots upward.
Kathleen is alone—no sleeping bag, no lantern, no
evidence of her husband except for the indentation in the
dead grass next to her.

"Kathleen!" comes her name again, and this
time, she clocks the direction. It's muffled, but it's there,
coming from the house, where the windows are alight
with a ruby glow. The smell of smoke hits her again. This
time, it's strong enough to scald the inside of her skull.

Our house is burning.

Hurling herself to her feet, Kathleen staggers toward the back steps. The knob burns to the touch—*locked.*

"Michael!" she calls, but her voice sounds garbled, caught somewhere between the voice in her head and the one she uses to speak. She tries again. *"Michael!"*

There's no answer. She'll have to break the door down. She steps back, bracing one shoulder forward like she's seen on those primetime police procedurals. Careening forward, her body collides with the wooden slab. She lands in a heap on the scratchy welcome mat.

Fire consumes it all.

The carpet, the shoes, the wallpaper, the wedding photos… they all burn around her, turning an inky black against the violent assault.

"Kathleen!"

The voice comes from above, but the stairs to the second floor are gone, replaced by an inferno that promises painful death to anyone foolish enough to try. But sure enough, if she listens closely, she hears the patter of feet above—like Michael is up there looking for her.

"Michael!" she strains over the fire's roar. *"I'm down here!"*

No response. *There's no other way.* Even so, her eyes still frantically search for another option. Somewhere straight ahead, glass bursts against the intolerable heat. She squints down the hall at a pair of doors, little windows shattered and frames crackling with embers…

That isn't right.

No, the French doors belong in the living room. Those should be around the corner, past the kitchen—not down the hall. Getting her bearings again, Kathleen turns around with a gasp that brands her lungs.

The door she burst through only moments ago is gone. In its stead stands the louvered frames of the pantry closet.

What's happening?

"Kathleen!"

Snapping her gaze up toward the sound of Michael's voice, Kathleen sees the ceiling give before it can collapse on her head. With a scream, she tears down the hall, falling debris decimating the path behind her. The ceramic knobs on the living room doors sear her palms as she rips them open, hurling herself inside. Desperate to steady herself, she catches her fingers on what feels like the edge of a table.

The kitchen?

Yes, that's where she is now, against all odds. With a delirious sort of awe, Kathleen watches the blaze consume her most comforting place, sink and dishrags awash with flames. But how could she be here when the kitchen is back the other way? It's as if someone has torn the blueprints of their house to pieces and papier-mâchéd them back together, entirely out of order.

I need to get out of here...

In the span of a blink, the wall that once hosted the blackened shapes of their cozy breakfast nook is now laid bare, save for another door.

Another door where there shouldn't be one.

She recognizes the wreath. The front door stares back at her, eerily untouched by the flames that crowd around its frame. *Why isn't it burning?*

As soon as the thought crosses her mind, the ceiling above begins to groan. This place is going down, one way or another. The front door is right there, unlatched with its chain hanging loose like the hand of a friend reaching over a perilous cliffside. Three steps and the turn of a knob might mean Kathleen won't burn alive.

Three steps and the turn of a knob might mean that at least *one* of them would—

"Kathleen!"

Michael's voice shatters through her, bursting the window above the kitchen sink. She can't leave. She can't leave him behind. Ignoring the obvious escape, Kathleen rounds the corner. Room after room, door after door, she barrels through the splintering obstacle course of her home, not bothering to linger on any particular tragedy.

None of it matters if he's gone.

Shielding her head from the downpour of bubbling plaster, she weaves past another front door, reaching instead for a new pair of illusory French doors. It's like this for longer than Kathleen can understand, a liminal time and space where nothing matters except for the next door and the one after that.

Soon, Kathleen begins to believe that Michael's voice is getting closer.

Past the sliding closet doors, she stumbles over her own feet, landing in a heap on the scratchy welcome mat once again. With blistering hands, she pushes herself up to see—*finally*—the staircase. It looms above her, painted in thick, ominous smoke. All but the very top step is engulfed.

"Kathleen!"

He's up there. She's so close, but she stopped for a moment too long. The fire leaps from the walls to cling to her, reaching with spindly fingers to plant palmlike burns across her bare arms and legs. She swats the flames away with a scream, but they chase her up the stairs, smoldering fingernails scratching at her heels.

Were there always so many steps?

"Kathleen!"

With a wild burst of energy, Kathleen barrels into the upstairs bathroom, slamming the door behind her.

She falls with a *crunch* on the floor, scrambling toward the edge of the tub. Her cheek presses to the ice-cold ceramic, a shock turned instantly soothing. Through bleary eyes, she watches steam rise from her raw skin.

Safe for now.

It's uncertain if the roar of the ravenous fire is truly gone or if the ringing in her ears is merely drowning it out. With a groan, Kathleen lifts herself from the tile floor. The sight of blood startles her. Upon closer examination, little pieces of glass pepper her palms with red. *How…?*

The frames of Michael's glasses lay mangled at her knees, lenses shattered beneath her.

"Michael?" she calls.

There's no reply.

Blood pools in the lines of her palms. With a wince, she plucks the glass from her skin, brushing the more microscopic bits away on the hem of her shirt. Rising to her feet, Kathleen doesn't have the chance to catch her breath before it jams tight in her throat.

"Michael?"

And there he is, staring back at her in the mirror. Tears prick in her eyes. *He's safe.*

With a sigh, Michael raises a toothbrush to his mouth. It's only then that she notices her own reflection. In the mirror, she's not the bloody, soot-stained woman she knows herself to be, but the woman of just hours ago. That Kathleen brushes her teeth too, lost in thought. The couple is dressed for a night under the stars, wearing clothes they won't miss if the Dreaming claims—

The Dreaming.

It's only then that Kathleen understands. *I'm dreaming.* This is all a dream. The voice, the fire, the broken glass—it's all just a part of the process. She could cry with relief.

Michael spits into the sink, planting a soft kiss on his wife's temple before he heads for the door. *For the fire.*

"*Stop,*" she calls hopelessly, knowing he can't hear her. It's not real. Still, she wants Michael to be safe. She wants him to never leave their home, to never fall asleep, to never succumb to whatever terrible nightmare awaits him.

But Michael disappears into the hall. She almost follows him, peeking her head beyond the threshold. A wave of heat makes her eyes water. The stairs still burn, wood ebonizing in the furnace. The Michael in the mirror is gone.

She closes the bathroom door, just her and her reflection in this tiled room. The Kathleen in the mirror smooths lotion over her face, going through the nighttime motions—pausing only to trace the shape of her nose and the curve of her lips.

Imagining a snout and a snarl, Kathleen recalls.

She knows what comes next. It's surreal, watching herself take the scissors to her own hair. The snip is loud, echoing through the room. Kathleen instinctively reaches a hand behind her ear, curling the stunted strands around a finger.

"*Can you bring my glasses down?*" Michael's voice calls from below, unworried.

"*Okay,*" both Kathleens reply.

Into the drawer, the loose lock goes. Without another glance at herself, Kathleen's reflection gathers her husband's unbroken glasses from the counter and leaves. The door hangs ajar, tendrils of smoke creeping against the jamb.

"*Sweet dreams,*" she calls after Mirror Kathleen with a breathless laugh. For all she knows, *she* could be Mirror Kathleen.

Curious what the Dreaming will show her next, she opens the drawer. There it is—the silky loop of hair waiting for her, open and inviting like an unblinking eye. With cracked fingers, she lifts the strands into the light.

It's red. Fire hydrant red. Or maybe, raw beef red. *Bloodred,* she decides.

The pigment seeps from the strands to stain her fingertips. Kathleen blinks her trickster eyes, but the story stays the same. The hair is still red, and now her fingers are too. A deep and powerful scarlet is blooming across her knuckles, wrists, and forearms, dying her pale flesh a ruddy sort of hue that seems to glow brighter and brighter with each passing second.

A thin plume of white smoke rises from the lock of hair, like someone's aimed a magnifying glass under a beam of sunlight. She shouldn't be surprised when it combusts between her fingers. She shouldn't be scared when the flames flutter down her arms, over her shoulders, up her neck, and into her mouth. Every aspect of this dream should have prepared her for the moment when her skin becomes the kindling.

But Kathleen is surprised, and she is scared. She's never felt fire on her skin like this, wicking up all the moisture, ravaging her flesh until it cracks wide open and disintegrates before her eyes. Dermis, epidermis, fat—it's all food to the flame. All she can do is watch in the mirror as the flames she thought she escaped swallow her whole.

I've gone and killed myself. Looking for Michael. Thinking I could save him.

Now, she'll die alone in a house fire, trapped on the second story—no escape. If she were to wake from this dream, maybe then she'd survive. But when she closes her eyes and accepts the pain, all she can see painted across her lids are flames…

"Kathleen!"

Her eyes snap open. There are two very cold hands cradling her face. She pushes away, flashes of red corrupting the otherwise gray scene. It smells like dawn, but Kathleen's mouth tastes like smoke. *Am I still dreaming?*

"Kathleen, it's okay. You're okay. We did it. Are you okay? Are you…?"

Kathleen meets Michael's eyes, registering his features as *friend,* not *foe.* "Michael?"

"Yes, my love." He sighs. "Are you hurt? You look…"

Her heart sinks. "I look…?"

He blinks at her, something like awe in the smile that dares to stretch across his face. Kathleen's chest tightens, like she is unable to take the suspense of it.

"You look the same," she blurts. "You look exactly the same. How do I…?" Her hoarse voice trails off when she lifts a hand to touch his face, flinching at the flash of *red.* Her hands. Her fingers. Even her cuticles.

All red.

Kathleen moans, distraught and exhausted. What does this mean? *Am I still dreaming?*

Michael wipes the tears from her cheeks—tears she didn't know had fallen. "Let's go inside," he says softly. "I don't know if you've noticed, but this cocoon shit smells like someone puked a matcha latte on a garbage fire."

For the first time, she notices the thin membrane that clings to Michael's stubble in patches. There are green chunks in his blond hair, and all around them are piles of gelatinous goop, verdant veins threaded throughout. Their sleeping bags, clothes, and all the grass around them for ten feet—gone.

"I had to dig myself out," he whispers. "Then I started on you. I hope I didn't wake you too soon. You looked so scared."

Kathleen shakes her head. "No—I—thank you."

"Look what survived," he muses, lifting his glasses to his eyes. "They're a little crooked. I think they got bent when we—"

Kathleen doesn't let him finish. She lunges for him, arms winding tight around his neck. His hug is reciprocal, as always, and Kathleen feels safe for the first time in weeks. They stay like that for a while before Michael suggests they go wash up.

"What is it?" he asks when Kathleen hesitates in the bathroom doorway.

"Nothing," she mutters, forcing herself to follow him. Inside, she keeps her head low, refusing to look at herself in the mirror. Half of her is scared to see the Kathleen from her dreams trapped in some sort of loop where the unknown hangs, guillotine-like, above her head. The other half—*more than half*—is dreading her transformation. The *unknown* waits for her, inches from her periphery, and she's too scared to look it in the face.

"Kathleen…" Michael tucks his thumb under her chin, lifting her eyes. "Look. You're beautiful."

With a sigh, Kathleen does what she's told. In the soft glow of the bathroom, Kathleen's skin seems to burn like a light source in and of itself. Her skin is red, but that's to be expected. It's her hair that really surprises her. It's darker than it ever was, her once chestnut-brown locks turned into a deep crimson, several shades darker than her flesh, almost black with a ruby sheen. Her eyes have changed too, a deep and wide furrow of red around her pupils—irises like a burning ring of fire.

"Is this real?" she wonders aloud.

"I think so."

"Do you feel any different?"

He scrutinizes his own reflection. "I don't think so," he decides.

Under the stream of the shower, Kathleen and Michael fall back on their usual patterns. Kathleen cranks the heat, griping about the old pipes, while Michael lets the scalding water turn his pale skin pink. Michael notes that they're low on his shampoo, and Kathleen discovers the same about her conditioner. They decide to go to the store this weekend, purposely ignoring reality in the name of staying sane.

After washing each other's bodies of all cocoon debris, they hold each other close, Michael's cheek pressed to the top of Kathleen's head.

"This may be the worst sunburn I've ever had," she breathes. Michael chuckles. *Good.* Her jokes are always for his benefit—even now. *Can't have him worrying too much about me.*

"You're so warm," he sighs. *You're the same*, she wants to say. *You're exactly the same.*

Chapter 7

Eggs have never tasted this good, piping hot with the creamiest yolks. Kathleen's eyelids flutter closed as she sighs. Moments ago, her husband offered her breakfast with a kiss on the cheek before he retreated into the living room, phone tucked against his ear.

"We don't know anything yet," he says in a low voice, pacing by the windows.

It's his mother. Kathleen knows this because Patricia would have her son call her every morning if she had a say. It doesn't even have to be a holiday; the Wiseman matriarch expects her loyal heir to call at least once a week or there is hell to pay. Michael's connection with his mother has always been a foreign thing to Kathleen as a woman who's spent most of her life without one. This morning, however, she understands. It's a nationwide crisis they're in, after all.

The Dreaming spans nearly every channel, only commercials and soap operas surviving the information frenzy. It's a real free-for-all out there with such limited understanding circulating the usual avenues. Several anchors are missing from their usual pixels on their television screen, reportedly *affected* by this unprecedented condition sweeping the nation. Some personalities still argue the truth of it, demanding that the average layperson not believe a word of what they hear from the media. Others are already focusing on damage control, insisting that the best scientists are on it, calling it by its new name.

"In the meantime," Nancy, the BBC presenter, says, looking prim as ever, "the World Health Organization continues to insist that all affected by *acute metamorphic oneirosis* stay home in an effort to mitigate the spread to coworkers and neighbors." Her usual co-presenter is nowhere to be seen—likely *affected.* "Next up, how to tell if you've been exposed to AMO. Take the assessment designed by the World Health Organization..."

Kathleen lowers the volume. She doesn't need an assessment to know that she's been changed by the Dreaming. When she woke with a start after only a couple hours of scattered sleep, she confirmed it. Every inch of her is red, from her scalp to the soles of her feet. Michael, meanwhile, seems completely the same. Actually, he'd seemed more himself than ever when she discovered him in the kitchen, making their breakfast.

"... just looks a little different..." he now says from behind the cracked double doors.

She strains to hear him more clearly. *Are they talking about me?*

"... no, I'm staying right here. She's my wife."

A primal sort of fear crawls into her throat. Patricia wants Michael to leave, to come and stay with her and Duke. It's testament to a reality that she could've gone her whole life without remembering, given the choice.

Loved ones can leave you at any moment.

She hasn't thought that way in a long time. Not since tumult became routine and cold shoulders became warm embraces. Shaking it off, Kathleen carries her plate to the sink, cranking the water on. It's surreal to so vividly remember this very sink consumed in flames. *But that wasn't real.* It was just the Dreaming distracting her as it rearranged her DNA.

Michael told her about his dream once they were properly de-slimed and snuggled beneath the covers. The sun was just starting to rise, outlining the profile of her husband's face as he remembered. It had taken him to the shop, but rather than have him wander an endless labyrinth, the Dreaming inflicted a different sort of powerlessness. Michael was strapped to the workshop table, magnifying glasses hovering over his naked body, wielded by shadowy assailants. He could hear Kathleen looking for him, but every time he struggled against his restraints, the grinder and torches would roar to life, promising torturous pain.

"I could just see their eyes, staring at me," he said with a shudder. "But I realized if I just let them look without trying to escape, they wouldn't threaten me. I decided, *If I can just get out of this alive, then I'll find Kathleen.*"

"Were you scared?"

He thought about it, adjusting the pillow under his cheek. "Yes and no. There was something kind of freeing about the lack of control. There was nothing to hide because hiding simply wasn't an option."

When Michael joins her in the kitchen again, Kathleen has her head buried in the cabinet under the sink, poking at the pipes.

"What's the matter?" he asks.

"The water isn't getting hot enough. We may need to call the plumber."

"Really?" The faucet turns on with a hiss. "Feels fine to me."

Kathleen lifts her head from the cabinets. "What did Patricia have to say?"

"Their private doctor is refusing to see them. Dad's heart is acting up, but the doctor says it isn't safe for them if he visits as usual."

"Has the doctor…?"

"That's my guess. Or he may just be quarantining for quarantine's sake."

"Is your mom denying that the Dreaming is happening? You can just send her a picture of me. I'd love to hear her try and deny *this*." She lifts a red hand, splaying her fingers wide.

Michael chuckles, catching her hand in his. "No, she's not denying it. She must think that she's somehow above it all, I s'pose. I told her to stay indoors for the time being."

"I'm sure she loved that."

He just smiles in response, leaning against the counter with a thoughtful expression.

Outside, a dog barks. Kathleen climbs to her feet to look out the kitchen window. Next door, their neighbor stands in his front yard as Roscoe the terrier scampers through the grass. One hand is buried in his hoodie pocket while the other thumbs at his phone. Kathleen doesn't notice anything out of the ordinary until he follows after his scruffy companion. His knees seem to bend backwards—those sweatpants looking less and less like pants and more and more like…

Fur.

"Randall has hooves," she says absently.

Michael peers out the window with her. "Would you look at that…"

Their hands stay intertwined on the sink ledge as they spy on their neighbor, who appears to have just stepped right out of a C.S. Lewis novel.

"I think we should go in today," she says suddenly.

"What?"

"To work. We should go in."

"Kathleen…"

"It's already spread to Thistle Grove. There's no stopping it. And besides, I feel fine. I feel the same. Nothing has changed except for how I look. We can't stop functioning in the world just because our appearances have changed—well, *my* appearance at least."

Michael releases her hand to rub her upper arms. "I just think we need to give it some time before we go out into the world and potentially cause more damage."

Damage. She tries not to react to that description of her condition. "You haven't changed at all. So why don't you just go in?"

"I don't want to leave you."

"Then I'll go in with you."

Kathleen's phone buzzes on the table. *Diana Hubbard*, the caller ID reads.

"Hi," she answers breathlessly. "Are you okay?"

"I think so," her friend says, but the tremor in her voice betrays her. "Can I see you?"

"Of course. Michael and I are just heading in."

After a prolonged look, Michael throws his hands up in surrender.

"Okay, good. I'm here already. I haven't seen anyone else yet. Um, Kathleen? When you see me… try not to be… too surprised."

"Promise. Same for you."

"I don't think anything could surprise me at this point."

Kathleen tries to be as discreet as possible, layering up more than what's reasonable for the temperate weather. Michael holds an umbrella over her face to and from the car, like a security detail for a high-profile celebrity. The idea of Michael as anyone's bodyguard makes her smile.

Joseph, Kathleen thinks. *We need to check on Joseph.*

Unlocking the door, she lowers her hat and sunglasses as she steps inside. A sliver of light from the entryway casts a glow across the maroon runner, and her eyes follow the trail up to a shadow behind the counter. There, her friend cowers, just a shape in the darkened room.

"Good lord." Diana gasps, clutching her chest. "You scared me." From the looks of it, she wears long sleeves and a winter beanie pulled down over her eyebrows.

"Diana?"

"Let's get some light in here, yeah?" Michael says gently, already reaching for the switch.

Diana laughs nervously. "If you insist."

The lights flicker on, and Diana flinches—at the change in atmosphere maybe, or more likely at Kathleen's appearance. She can't find it in herself to be offended because looking at Diana is like looking in a funhouse mirror. Under the swathes of knit fabrics, Diana seems exactly as she was—*no snout, no snarl.* Only where Kathleen is shades of red, Diana is shades of blue. Her eyes, once a milk chocolate brown, are an eerily vibrant cobalt. She pulls her hat off to reveal her once brunette hair turned a gleaming navy.

"You're red," Diana says simply.

"You're blue," Kathleen returns.

Diana narrows her eyes at Michael. "How come he's the same?"

"We're not sure," Michael says. "For all we know, I might not be."

Her new blue eyes widen. "You mean…?"

"It might not be physical," Kathleen explains. "We just don't know yet. How about you? Do you feel okay?"

"Besides looking like Violet Beauregard's estranged aunt?" Diana scoffs.

Kathleen snorts in response. Her friend's eyes flare.

"Don't laugh," she pleads.

"I'm sorry. Do you feel okay? Like on the inside?"

Diana shrugs, exasperated. "I guess! For all I know, my insides are blue too. That can't be healthy. And how am I supposed to see my girls when I look like *this*? Like I just stepped out of a bad science experiment? I could barely muster up the courage to come here this morning. How am I supposed to pick my girls up at Eric's? *God!*"

"Hey, it's okay. We'll figure it out." With careful steps, Kathleen joins Diana behind the counter. "Just breathe."

"And no one's heard from Joseph or Travis yet?" Michael asks, his phone in his hand.

Diana sniffles, shaking her head as she lowers her forehead to the counter. "It's all just a bad dream. A horrible, awful, no good, very bad dream…"

"Why don't you call Travis and I'll call Joseph?" Kathleen suggests, and Michael is already dialing.

"On it," he says, lifting his phone to his ear.

Meanwhile, Kathleen drapes an arm over her friend's shoulders as she listens to her own phone ring, running her hand back and forth across the wool fabric of Diana's sweater.

"Hello?"

"Joseph! It's Kathleen," she says. "Sorry, you probably knew that. Are you okay?"

His laugh is a strangled sort of sound. "Define *okay*."

"It sounds like you're alive and breathing."

"Yep." He sighs. "Got those two covered. How are you and Michael fairing?"

"Michael is perfectly okay. He didn't change at all. I… look a little different."

"Different how?"

She hasn't had to explain it to someone yet. "Um, my complexion and hair color has changed. Diana's too."

"You're with Diana?"

"We're at the shop."

"Well, I'm afraid to say that I don't think I'll be joining y'all at work this morning. I don't got any pants that fit."

"What do you mean?"

"Well, I don't got any pants that account for the tail."

Joseph has a tail? "Oh."

"Mary's working on it. She's already got the sewing machine out and running."

"Has she changed at all?"

"Yeah," he says, voice hoarse with dry humor. "Woke up with bigger ears to listen better to all my grumbling. Other than the ears, she's stayed mostly the same."

Michael waves his phone at her, shaking his head. He mouths something Kathleen can't catch before exiting the shop, walking back to the car.

"Joseph, I've got to go," Kathleen says. "Don't worry about work today. None of us really know how to function in this new normal, so work is the lowest of priorities right now. Give us a call later, okay? You and Mary take care. Let me know if you need anything."

"Will do, Kathleen. You and Michael take care too."

"Bye now."

When Kathleen hangs up, it seems Diana's condition has mellowed somewhat. She stares blankly ahead, the tears all but gone except for the shiny tracks on her cheeks.

"Where did Michael go just now?" Kathleen asks.

"To check on Travis. He's not picking up."

"Really?" *Maybe the Dreaming took his hands.* Kathleen thinks better of cracking that joke with this audience. "Let's lock up and wait in the office. Does that sound okay?"

It takes a little convincing, but soon the two are cozied up in the office with fresh cups of coffee. Kathleen sucks hers down in a minute flat while Diana waits for hers to cool.

"What did you dream about?" her friend whispers.

Kathleen shudders. "Our house was burning down. I could hear Michael inside, calling for me. But the layout was all wrong—the rooms all mixed up. I couldn't find him. I ran through door after door until I finally shut myself in the bathroom. From there on, it's a little fuzzy. The fire caught up to me. I remember that."

Diana nods, a haunted look hanging from her hollow gaze. "I was outside. Middle of freaking nowhere. It was cold and dark. The only lights were these streetlamps behind me. But I had this feeling that my girls were lost somewhere out there, like an intuition, I guess. So I didn't walk toward the lights. I kept trudging out into this field, trying to find my girls and take them home with me. Didn't even realize I'd been walking on ice until it broke under me. The water… It all felt so real."

"Mine too."

Silence falls over them like an emergency blanket—a small comfort of commiseration. While Diana quietly disassociates next to her, Kathleen turns her attention back to the internet.

"Look," Kathleen says, pointing at the screen. "Someone has started cataloging the different types of transformations that have been recorded across the world."

Diana blinks slowly, reading. *"The Dreaming: Species Com-pen-di-um.* It can't be a *species* compendi—compend—whatever. We're all human."

"Well, maybe not anymore."

Diana moans, burying her face in her hands. "Oh god…"

Claws, beaks, fur, wings… Kathleen stops scrolling when her eyes stutter over a species type under the *rare* subcategory.

"'Jinns,'" she reads aloud. "'are magical beings. Their eyes, hair, and skin color take on an inhuman hue. Besides the superficial aspects, their physicality remains—'"

"I wouldn't call this *superficial,*" Diana mutters.

"'—humanlike. Little is known about jinns. In Arabic mythologies, they are known to grant wishes, otherwise known as *genies* or, in Western adaptations, *a genie in a bottle.* How jinns grant wishes and what other abilities they may exert are still unknown. If you or someone you know has the appearance of a jinn, please contact the Arcane Archivist to—'"

"Arcane Archivist? This can't be real."

"It's the name of the website," Kathleen defends. "Doesn't that sound like us though? Only the surface level changes, nothing substantial—"

Diana lifts her face, now almost purplish with frustration. "Nothing substantial?"

"I'm just saying that this might be the first step to some answers."

"The only answer I need is how to reverse this."

"Well, if we really are jinns, we can grant wishes."

Diana scoffs, glaring. "Like Genie? From *Aladdin*?

"Your complexion certainly fits the bill," Kathleen teases half-heartedly.

"Okay, Jafar," Diana snaps.

"I'm being serious," Kathleen insists, surprising herself by how serious she really is. "Make a wish. Maybe I can grant it or you can grant it yourself."

Diana rolls her eyes. "I wish to go back to normal."

The clock ticks as empty seconds roll by.

"Try holding my hands," Kathleen prompts. "And close your eyes."

"Are you for real?"

"Just do it."

Diana does what she's told, but not before some grumbling. With her hands clasped tightly in Kathleen's, she closes her eyes. "I wish that my sweet, crazy friend Kathleen and I could go back to normal."

Kathleen closes her eyes too. Diana's hands are freezing to the touch, so cold that her fingers start to ache the longer she holds them. Diana is the first to rip her hands free, though.

"Girl, why are your hands so hot? You're like a furnace!"

"And yours are like ice cubes." A light, almost imperceptible steam rises in between them, like a pot left to boil on an early winter's morning.

"Well, I think we can cross *jinn* off the list of possibilities. You're still a red hot and I'm still a blueberry, so…"

This time, when Kathleen bursts into laughter, Diana isn't too reluctant to join her. They're both keeled over with giggles when Kathleen's phone buzzes on the desk.

"Hello?" Kathleen sighs pleasantly as Diana wipes tears from her eyes.

At first, only the sound of sirens can be heard on the other end.

Kathleen leans forward, tucking her phone more securely against her ear. "Hello? Michael, are you there?"

His sob rips through her like a bullet. "Travis didn't make it. He didn't—"

"Travis… what?"

"—I called the cops. He's—oh *god*, Kathleen. He's half-turned, but, but, he's—he didn't survive. I found him in his bunker. He's *dead*, Kathleen."

Visions of Travis's lifeless form saturate Kathleen's imagination. She's never seen the inside of his bunker, but she imagines it's as cold and lifeless as his body must be. *Oh, Travis.*

Diana grips Kathleen's sleeve, eyes demanding more information. Kathleen only shakes her head in response, her lungs seized with panic—voiceless. The first victim of the Dreaming in Thistle Grove is Michael's childhood friend, discovered by none other than the jewelry shop owner himself.

While I sat here and laughed with my *childhood friend.*

"Michael, I'm so sorry," she chokes out. "I'm so sorry."

Kathleen's eyes blur with hot tears as she stares straight ahead, words about *magic* and *wishes* glaring back at her from the computer screen. She wants to break the screen in half. Answers aren't answers at all in this new and terrible landscape. *There are only more questions.*

Chapter 8

It just so happens that the first community event since the Dreaming is a funeral.

Attendance is light. It's not like Travis was the town pariah or anything, though anyone with a bunker in their backyard warrants a bit of neighborly leeriness. He was a legend at the local watering hole's trivia night. He was a regular at the bait and snare shop. He volunteered every fall to drain his neighbors' hoses before the first snow. Travis Simms was no recluse.

The funeral isn't well attended because of the Dreaming. Many opted to stay home to quarantine from those changed, to avoid changing others, or to merely reject their new reality.

It seems like an illustration from a children's book, this array of bizarre attendees under the church's steeple. Tails, tusks, and talons—their owners are all gathered in various stages of funeral discretion to mourn and remember. To gawk and whisper.

Pastor Dolton is a lizard person. His face is no longer humanoid, those naturally wide-set eyes now wider apart than they once were, set atop a very reptilian snout. His melanated skin has taken on a richly teal pigment. Kathleen estimates that he stands nearly a foot taller than he once did, towering over the podium in his newly tailored pastoral robes.

"We are gathered here today to mourn the loss of a beloved resident of Thistle Grove," he says, his voice deeper and richer than ever. "Travis Simms—brother, uncle, and friend…"

"He'd hate this," Michael mutters next to her. He bounces his knee, and the whole pew shivers with him. His nose is raw, victim to the cheap tissues balled up in his fist. She puts a hand on his knee in silent agreement.

"In these trying times," Pastor Dolton continues, "tragedy can get lost in the tumult. I thank each and every one of you for attending this solemn affair, not just for our friend's sake, but for the sake of our community. We must band together. Changed or otherwise, we are still children of God. To begin, a passage from Psalms…"

The casket is closed and for good reason. Michael said that when he found Travis, the man had begun a werewolf-like transformation—his tawny beard turning into dark fur and his green eyes into two red bulges. Before it turned the dexterous hands of their prized repair technician into bumbling paws, the Dreaming disqualified Travis from this strange new world.

Kathleen sucks in a quiet breath. *Why did he have to die when all of us lived?*

She tries not to stare; she really does. Every time she finds herself looking, she catches someone else staring right back at her. No one changed quite like Kathleen or Diana, so they inspire a lot of strange looks from the other churchgoers. This time, she catches the eye of Lydia Moore—Travis's sister. She is a pale sprite of a thing with sharp cheekbones and haunted eyes. Lydia was always a small woman, the wings that spawn from the back of her navy-blue peacoat only emphasizing that smallness. Brown and gold in one light, gray and silver in another, Lydia's wings quiver like a butterfly's as she cries from crystalline eyes.

Kathleen tries to offer her a smile, but it feels more like a grimace. Whispers to her left are a necessary distraction.

"Pass them down," Diana insists, waving a gloved hand. She has employed the aid of Mary's sewing skills to create a few *staple pieces*, as she calls them. Kathleen can't help but think that the black veil obscuring her face is more of an occasion accessory than a staple.

How many funerals is Diana planning to attend?

Mary gives Kathleen a look of commiseration a little ways down the pew. She has elven ears now, just like Beth Jones. Rather than her ginger counterpart, however, Mary Thompson wears her gingerbread-colored locs up in a bun with a pair of gold hoop earrings. She passes something to her husband before leaning back in the pew, all but disappearing behind his massive frame. He sits very awkwardly on the bench to accommodate his tail. Peering around his elbow, Kathleen finally sees the object being passed: a crumpled pack of tissues. Joseph stares at the mundane thing, sitting doll-sized in his scaly, clawed hand.

How often does he do this? How often does he hold everyday objects, remembering what they felt like on his skin?

Everything must seem so small to him now, so weightless. He clenches the plastic pack in his palm, releases it, and watches as the tissues inflate back into shape.

For as little as Mary changed, Joseph seemed to bear the brunt of the Dreaming. Unlike Pastor Dolton, Joseph's reptilian scales are a true green, gleaming like emeralds against his black suit, swaths of fabric added to account for his growth. When he turns to hand Kathleen the tissues, his tail bumps her knee.

"Sorry, still getting used to that," he grumbles quietly. "Here."

"Thank you," she whispers.

Michael makes quick use of Diana's tissues, and by the time the service has ended, he's carrying one of the church-provided tissue boxes against his chest like an oath to his grief.

"We should talk to Lydia." He sniffles. "See how she's holding up."

They do, but not until they're gathered at the cemetery, standing over the freshly tilled earth where the coffin was laid to rest. After Michael pays his tearful respects to Travis's sister, he retreats to the car. Kathleen remains at the site with Lydia, who stares hollow-eyed at the tombstone.

Travis Simms — 1983-2020
Loved by His Family and Friends

"The stone is beautiful," she tries.

Lydia scoffs. "He'd hate it. He would've preferred cremation. But it's not like he put it in writing. I mean, he was so young when he… Who is giving any serious thought to their last wishes when they're only 37 years old? He's not even in there, you know."

"What do you mean?"

"I signed his remains over to the investigators. They wanted to do some research, run some tests. If Travis's death can serve a purpose, maybe even help some people, then it's just what we have to do." She wipes a stray tear from her pale cheek. "I think David hates me for it."

Kathleen dredges the name from her memories— David is her son. *Travis's nephew.* She can't recall if they were close. "Why would he? The decision was yours to make."

Lydia gives her a look that would be harsh if it weren't on the edges of red-rimmed eyes. "Are you serious? I basically signed my little brother over to the very government he hates."

Kathleen softens. "Yeah, he probably wouldn't have approved. But I understand why you did what you did. You were thinking about all the people he could help."

Lydia sighs. "Being a nurse makes you think about bodies differently. They're only a part of who we are—or *were*. Systems that need maintaining. Systems that fail." Her wings flutter a bit in the breeze. "David's at that age where it feels like the whole world is against him."

Kathleen looks around, realizing she hasn't seen him yet today. "Is he at school?"

Lydia barks a laugh. "Who knows? I woke up one morning with goddamn fairy wings and a missing teenager. The only evidence that he hasn't vanished into thin air is the state of our pantry. Wherever he's hiding out these days, he still comes back for food."

Kathleen swallows her discomfort. *What do I know about raising a teenager?* "At least he's eating. We're here if you need anything, Lydia. Food, company, financial support. Whatever you need. Please don't hesitate to ask."

Lydia nods, drawing Kathleen into her arms. She returns the hug with quiet intensity, feeling exactly how frail the tiny woman really is. This peacoat does a good job of hiding Lydia's skin and bones. Kathleen's eyes sting with fresh tears.

"I'll come by the shop to pick up his things," Lydia says, her voice tight. "He loved his work, Kathleen. He loved you both. You know that."

"Yeah, I know," she murmurs back, squeezing tighter. The woman's wings flutter back and forth, obscuring the gravestone with brilliant shimmers of light before Kathleen's teary eyes. It's downright mesmerizing. Even after she lets Lydia go, a slight aura of prismatic color lingers in Kathleen's field of vision, hovering over the gravesite just to Lydia's left.

When she gets into the car, Michael smiles for the first time in days.

"I'm glad you talked to her for a while," he says. "I just couldn't keep it together. Lydia's like a sister to me and—" He cuts himself off, taking a shuddering breath. "I'm just glad you talked to her. Thank you."

"I was happy to. We'll check in with her again soon," Kathleen promises.

From here, that strange iridescence that seems to follow Lydia's steps looks more like a smudge on the window and less like a magical aura. She almost asks Michael if he can see it too, but they're already turning onto the street, leaving the cemetery in the rearview window.

Tradition in mind, the surviving Jenkins' Jewelers employees convene at Madame Butterfried's for deep fried comforts and commemoration.

"Five jelly donuts, three cups of coffee, and two cups of tea," Hilary says, passing their orders across the booth. Kathleen can't help but admire the transformation of the diner's beloved owner. Long whiskers frame her newly pointed face, and a thick coat of soft white fur contrasts her honey-colored uniform. Her fingers taper into claws that perch on her hips now, leaving slight impressions on her apron.

"Thank you," Kathleen says, accepting a donut and one of the cups of tea. The second goes to Mary, who smiles up at Hilary.

"How are you doing, Hilary?" she asks.

"Oh, you know." The owner sighs. "Losing Travis is…" She blinks back the tears in her slitted eyes, and Kathleen could swear that she sees a cloudy form hovering in the air behind her. *Almost like a tail.* "It's rough. I wish he were here. Travis always had my back. I swear, if one more person calls me a *foxy* lady, I'll lose it."

They all laugh, but it's a hollow sound. With a few parting words, Hilary retreats to the kitchen, wiping her eyes on the back of her hand, that spectral tail following her.

"Is anyone else's coffee lukewarm?" Diana asks.

Michael and Joseph shake their heads, steam visibly rising from their mugs.

"Ugh, I swear I haven't had a hot cup of coffee in days."

Kathleen spots a couple of waitresses whispering around the coffeemaker. One looks unchanged from this distance, and the other's vibrant green hair could simply be the work of the local salon. "I can go ask someone to top you off."

"No, no, it's fine." Diana harumphs.

"These really are the best," Michael mumbles around a mouthful of powdered sugar and preserves. "I get why he was so territorial about them."

Mary smiles. "Food is always better when it's associated with a memory. Travis would always send Joseph home with venison jerky after a hunting trip."

"Whew, those were good," Joseph recalls. "He always wanted me to go hunting with him, but I never did. I don't regret that—the man was intense *without* a firearm. I wish I'd given him more of a chance though. Wish I'd given him the time of day."

"He wasn't the easiest person to be friends with," Michael admits. "But there was no one like him. He's the whole reason Kathleen and I even considered becoming jewelers. Without Travis's skillset, I don't think we would have—"

Something clatters in the kitchen. Joseph moves to applaud the mishap, as is diner tradition, but halts when a scream rips through the establishment.

"Get *OUT* of here!"

Hilary is just barely visible through the serving hatch, whipping a metal bowl at the ground. The two waitresses scurry to the far corner of the diner, huddling behind the jukebox. The usual diner hum of conversation and plate clinking quiets to an eerie silence.

Just as Michael and Joseph stand, Hilary whips her hand around to point at them.

"Stay where you are! I've got this!" Her gaze drops again, a furious line of fire at whatever poor pest has managed to wander into the wrong kitchen. "*Demon...*"

The door to the kitchen swings open, and what scurries out into the diner proper is not at all what Kathleen expects. Standing at about two feet tall, a green-skinned creature skulks across the tiled floor, flashing fangs full of kitchen scraps. It looks almost like a human child, impish in size but utterly horrifying in presence. Its eyes bounce feverishly from plate to plate.

"What *is* that thing?" Diana whispers, melting deeper into the booth.

It whips its too-large head around to stare at them with rabid, sunken eyes. All Kathleen can see in them is primal *hunger*. It's like there isn't a single thought behind them besides the appetite. Foam clings to the edges of its mouth, dripping to the floor in puddles.

"Do *not* give that little shit any food," Hilary demands, emerging from the kitchen with a push broom. "Michael, sweetie, would you get that door?"

Michael rips the front door open, letting the spring breeze into the charged room.

"Stand back," she orders before setting her sights on the creature. "Now, *git!*"

Armed with her impromptu weapon, Hilary forces the intruder from the establishment, her cloudy tail twitching with every firm thwack of the broom. Michael swings the door shut behind it, drowning out its anguished cries as it retreats into the alley. Hilary calms her panting before turning to face her horrified customers.

"Sorry for the drama, folks," she calls out. "We've got a real problem with those things lately. Exterminators are here next week. Again, really sorry for the disruption. Carry on."

Michael joins them back at the booth, eyes wide. "What was that thing?"

"Something straight out of hell," Diana squeaks. "It better not get into the shop."

Mary sighs to herself. "I wonder who that was."

"Do you mean…?" Kathleen asks, barely daring to finish the thought.

"Another product of the Dreaming," Mary says with a solemn nod. "I'm certain of it."

"How do you know?" Diana whispers.

"You ever seen one around here before the Dreaming? That was somebody to someone. Unfortunately, their transformation was a bit more substantial than most."

"Than *some*," Joseph mumbles. His claws are coated in sugar, congealed with jelly.

"Than some." With gentle hands, Mary uses a napkin to wipe the mess from her lover's hands. It's so tender that Kathleen looks away, embarrassed to intrude on such a private moment. Her own donut sits untouched on its doily. She doesn't have much of an appetite anymore.

"Anyone want to finish mine?"

"Pass it here," Michael says. Holding the donut aloft for all their circle to see, he clears his throat. "To Travis. May that fool rest in the peace he deserves. May there always be fish on his hook and jelly donuts in his lunch box."

The remaining sips of their coffee and scraps of their donuts join the toast.

"To Travis!"

Chapter 9

"It's something straight out of a Tolkien novel. If you would have told me that the guy who delivers my mail would show up one day as a living and breathing orc, I would have told you to go screw yourself. The man's hideous now—and Carl, let me tell you, it's such a shame because he used to be a nice-looking guy…"

Kathleen thumbs down the volume on the radio as she toes the bathwater. It used to be a weekly ritual, taking a bath to calm her nerves at the end of a long week. It's been a while since she's allowed herself the luxury. It doesn't help that seeing her bare skin is still a shock. She pours a little extra bubble mix into the water for that very reason.

"We are lucky," the other host says, presumably Carl. "We've remained *people*, for starters. Not everyone has been so fortunate. My wife, God bless her, has a beak."

"A beak?"

"She's a whole bird now, Cary. Wings, talons, beak."

"I'm sorry, man. That's unbelievable." Cary sighs, true remorse in his voice.

"You know, only a small percentage of us have stayed human. It's a rarity. What do you think it means?"

"That we ate our vegetables?"

Their laughter is empty and performative. Kathleen scoffs as she lowers herself into the bath. This isn't exactly the type of program she'd normally tune into. Frankly, she finds these personalities very annoying. Not many reputable stations allow amateur theorizing on their air waves for fear of spreading misinformation. Kathleen, however, is ravenous for *any* information she can get.

"Rat people, fox people, lizard people—we've got the whole animal kingdom represented at the station. It's a veritable zoo out here," Cary says. "Everyone's retained their mental faculties, thank Christ. Can you imagine if your wife became truly birdbrained?"

"Hey, I didn't say that she wasn't a little empty in the head to begin with."

They laugh again, and Kathleen hisses in disgust.

"Should people be wary of any particular species—can we call them *species*?"

"What else are we supposed to call them?"

Carl snorts. "I don't know, *creatures?*"

"Creatures, species, it's all the same to me. It's the goblins you've gotta worry about. They're infiltrating our homes to steal our food. One broke into mine last week! It ate through our entire pantry before we found it—get this—trapped in the fridge. It's like its whole personality is its appetite, and—I'll say it—that's a pretty dangerous motivation."

"Right! What if they start eating our pets next? Our *kids?*"

"It's truly monstrous what AMO has done to some people. Can't call them people anymore, can we? Not when they are little green men gobblin' up—"

"Gobblin'! There's some etymology for you—
gobblin' goblins!"

Kathleen cuts the laughter short, snatching the
radio off the sink. Cary's raspy voice still scratches at her
mind.

"It's the goblins you've gotta worry about…"

The eyes of that tiny, rageful creature have
haunted Kathleen ever since that day at the diner. Was
there a spark of intelligence in them, or was that just the
root of the hunger? The gnawing ache? What makes a
person like that? Theories of *who* becomes *what* have
begun to circulate, and Kathleen's entire news feed is full
of clickbait.

*Why do I have fur but you have feathers?
Personalities might influence transformations.*

*Why is it a "race" thing? Geneticists speculate
the DNA of the Dreaming.*

*What does your occupation say about your
transformation? Take the quiz!*

She put her phone down over an hour ago, but
her eyelids are still stamped with the bold fonts and
bizarre stock photos. Sinking into the bubbles, Kathleen
takes a deep breath before letting the water crest over her
forehead.

It's quiet here. No more boisterous talk show
voices. No more carnival barker headlines.

Instead, her mind echoes with the hymn sung at
Travis's funeral, so familiar to her.

*Abide with me: fast falls the eventide;
the darkness deepens; Lord, with me abide.
When other helpers fail and comforts flee,
Help of the helpless, O abide with me…*

The last time she sang that hymn was many, many
years ago.

"Come on," her grandmother said, pulling her up from the pew. *"Get on your feet. Sing."*

Kathleen can still taste her tears as she followed along on the gilded page that day.

Swift to its close ebbs out life's little day;
Earth's joys grow dim, its glories pass away...

Her memory skips the blurry parts—the condolences, the *I'm so sorry for your loss*es, the looks of pity around every corner. What is clear to her are those two freshly laid graves, rainwater filling the muddy divot between them.

"It's unimaginable," Lucille said to another mourner, a personal raincloud clinging to her lips. Her grandmother always had a pack of smokes in her left coat pocket, an old Zippo tucked in the right. She was on her fifth of the day, if Kathleen counted correctly. *"It isn't right. No one should outlive their kid. Your parents dying before you? Now, that's natural. That makes sense. She'll grow out of it, but what am I supposed to do?"*

Kathleen clings to the edge of the tub, gasping for breath. She'd nearly blacked out, held hostage under the water by that heavy memory. Above the surface, steam coats the room like a weighted blanket. With shaky legs, she steps out of the tub, reaching for the exhaust switch. A dark spot obscures her vision, floating down her arm like a spider lazily weaving its web.

Too hot, she thinks. *I should sit down...*

She tries to blink it away, but the spot is persistent. It stretches and coils around her arm, snakelike now. Kathleen has lost consciousness before, but this isn't like that. The tendrils nestle into the crook of her elbow, and from the inky void comes a shape—the shape of...

Pipe organ fills her ears once again, but this time she can feel the vibrations in her bones.

"Nervous?" Diana asks, linking her arm in Kathleen's. The rosy color of her gown cuddles in close with the white tulle of Kathleen's wedding dress.

"Only about this veil," Kathleen hears herself grumble, adjusting the lace for the fifth time. *"How does anyone see with one of these on?"*

"You don't have to wear it. Quick, turn around." With deft fingers, Diana unclips the veil from Kathleen's hair, taming a few flyaways in the process. *"Better?"*

"Much. Patricia is going to have some words."

"Well, it's not Patricia's day, is it?"

"Try telling her that."

The two swallow their snickers as the music shifts behind the stained-glass doors.

"Thank you for this," Kathleen whispers. *"I know it's unconventional, but—"*

"If your dad were here, I'd probably still fight for this. I'm honored to walk you down the aisle. No one's ever getting between my Katy and me."

Just then, the double doors open to a blindingly bright light…

Kathleen slams one hand on the sink's edge, catching herself before she falls.

What's happening?

That was her wedding day—everything exactly as she remembers it to be. The itchy veil, the laughably loud music, her best friend on her arm where her father couldn't be. It was all right before her in real time. *But how…?*

Another dark spot chases her vision, sneaking over her left wrist and up her fingers. She tries to wipe it away, gasping as it stains her fingertips—this time with a different shape altogether. This time with a memory she'd thought she'd long forgotten.

The hospital lights dull the red pastel in Kathleen's hand. The tree outside her bedroom window has the prettiest fall leaves, and once she finishes its likeness, the portrait of their family home will be complete. She'd started it back at the kitchen table this morning, and Dad loved the look of it so much that he'd promised to put it up in his office.

"Mrs. Demsky?" a surgeon asks from the doorway, specks of red on her scrubs. Seeing Kathleen, she retreats partially behind the door. *Hiding the blood.*

"She's outside," Kathleen says.

The young surgeon nods, chewing on her lower lip before smiling softly. *"Well, when she comes back, let her know that we would like to speak with her."*

"You can just tell me. They're my parents," Kathleen argues, voice squeezing past the lump in her throat.

Her eyes are sympathetic. *"Let's wait."*

It's then that Kathleen knows that her parents are dead. The car crash they endured earlier that rainy evening had killed them in the end. Lucille returns to find her crying over her pastels, ruining them. It was the last time her grandmother ever held her like she really meant it.

When Kathleen comes to, she's kneeling on the bathroom floor, hands clinging to the counter's edge. Her body is covered in these black markings now, shimmering like oil on water. She's too weak to look away, watching an intricate design coil around her hips, settling just below her belly button...

Suddenly, Kathleen is sitting in their first apartment's bathroom, ten weeks pregnant. The spotting in her underwear is alarming, but not necessarily bad if she remembers correctly. She flips open her phone and dials the clinic right then and there, describing the stains to the nurse practitioner in detail. She makes an appointment for the next morning.

When they can't find a heartbeat, they give her misoprostol, painkillers, and sad smiles.

"It's very normal for first-time mothers to miscarry," the nurse says.

Kathleen squeezes her eyes closed. *Please. Not these memories.*

When she opens them, she is back in the bathroom, but this time in their apartment on Burrow Street. On the wall hangs dried bouquets—one from her own wedding and one from Diana's the year after. Just across the hall hangs a picture of Haley, Diana's firstborn, sleeping soundly in a basket of fresh linens.

Kathleen is nine weeks along. This time, the dark spots on her underwear taunt her. More spots mean more misoprostol. More horrendous pain. More blood clots that make her dizzy to look at. *Baby Blue* is gone within a week of beginning treatments.

No, no, no, no, no…

She shakes her head free of this memory, only managing to catapult herself into the next.

Now, her head is in a bucket lined with vomit. The toilet seat is cold against her thighs. For the third time in her life, medicine expels the cells of her latest attempt at motherhood. This time, Kathleen is only eight weeks along when her baby's heart ceases to beat.

"It's okay, it's okay, it's okay," Michael repeats over and over again, rubbing warm circles on her back. The other times, she insisted on privacy—preserving the fragments of her dignity. This time, however, she needs him to understand. She needs him in the room with her.

"I'm sorry," she cries. *"I'm sorry."*

"Kathleen?"

When Kathleen wakes up, she's curled up on the bathroom floor. Her chest heaves with silent sobs as she tries to catch her breath. Her lungs feel too small—too tight.

There's a knock at the door.

"Kathleen? I heard something fall. I'm coming in," Michael says, opening the door. It bumps against her knee. "Oh my god, are you okay?" He squeezes through the crevice, careful not to step on her. "What happened? Are you hurt?"

"I'm sorry." She whimpers.

Michael scoops her into his arms, cradling her head against his shoulder. Her breath shudders in her chest as he rocks them back and forth. When her fingers feel strong enough, she clutches his sweater, and when her breath feels big enough, she wails like a child.

Michael holds her like that for a while. Kathleen can't be sure how long. She doesn't even remember him wrapping her in both of their towels, cocooning her in terrycloth.

"Can you tell me what happened?" he asks eventually.

She shakes her head. How could she? How could she even begin to explain what she just experienced? Pulling one arm free, she reaches up to the light.

"What do you see?"

He considers a moment before taking her forearm in his hand, running his thumb along the inscrutable tattoos that now decorate her scarlet skin.

"I see… perfection." He presses a kiss to the top of her head. "A beautiful sunset." Another kiss. "The last embers of a bonfire." Another. "A glass of wine after a long day's work." He tilts her chin up. "I see my wife."

But you don't see the markings. You don't see that my entire life is etched into my skin.

"What do you see?" he returns.

Her voice is only a whisper. "Everything."

Chapter 10

Kathleen wakes to the tickle of Michael's stubble as he kisses her cheek.

"Hey," she grumbles, blinking at her husband—fully dressed, even shoes on his feet. "What's going on?"

"Mom called, and it sounds like they've had their own Dreaming."

Kathleen sits upright. "Are they okay?"

He nods. "They seem shaken up, but they both survived the night. I'm going to go check on them, see if they need anything. Just… see them." His voice is thin, like it could break at any second. Kathleen reaches her sleep-warmed hand for his cool one. He lifts it to press her open palm against his cheek. "So warm."

"Do you want me to come with?"

"I want you to stay in this warm bed until the last possible second. Diana's opening this week, right?"

Their friend had kindly taken on an extra week of opening alongside Joseph. Without Travis in rotation, there would be more work for all of them. They would need to hire a new technician sooner than anyone felt comfortable with.

"Yeah. I'll take care of things," Kathleen promises. She'll list the job online today.

He leaves her with another tender kiss. The front
door opens and closes, and Kathleen tries to fall back
asleep. Eventually, she gives up, throwing off the covers.
It's as good a time as any to start the day.

"You're early," Joseph remarks when Kathleen
walks into the shop, the bell obnoxiously announcing
her entrance. *Too loud.* Hoisting onto her tippy toes, she
grabs the brass to silence it. Joseph smirks, his elongated
face still so expressive.

"Couldn't sleep," she says.

The office door opens to the sound of Diana's
soft snores. The exhausted mother of three slumps over
the desk, a heavy sweater draped over her shoulders. Her
dark blue hair flies free from the hat it's been hostage
to for many days now, splayed across her forearms like
shimmering tributaries. Kathleen marvels at the color.
Like the ocean at night.

She closes the door quietly so as not to wake her
friend. Diana hasn't been sleeping well with the girls
away at Eric's—quarantining from her. Kathleen knows
this from all the texts she receives at odd hours. The latest
was around three this morning.

It read: *What do you think about "Likewise
Jewelers" for a new name? I'm not sure what it
means, but I think it's kind of cute. Everyone LIKES the
WISEmans!*

She never responded. Guilt sneaks behind her
heart like a misbehaving child hiding from reprimand.
Kathleen has been so preoccupied with her own
transformation that she has neglected her best friend's
difficulties. They are the only two like them in Thistle
Grove, and they need to stick together. If anyone is going
to understand what Diana is going through, it would be
Kathleen. *And vice versa.*

Peering at the rare slivers of icy blue skin that her friend has left exposed, Kathleen wonders if Diana has markings too. She circles the desk with light footsteps, careful not to bump into her. Leaning in, she scrutinizes the thin line of skin just above Diana's collar. Squinting her eyes, she searches for any sign of movement.

Diana sighs, shifting in her sleep.

Just when Kathleen is about to give up, there it is. One shimmering tendril layers on another and another and another until they form a solid pattern of black—*well, half of a pattern,* Kathleen thinks. *I can't see it all.* She almost lifts a hand to clear the hair away but thinks better of it. That's crossing a line.

A glimmer catches her eye at Diana's feet. Kathleen kneels to pick up a single ruby stud. The setting is identical to her own sapphires, and she reflexively reaches up to turn the one in her left earlobe.

I didn't know she had these.

At nose level is a run in Diana's black tights, spanning the bend of her knee. Through the strained threads, another shimmer catches Kathleen's eye. It feels intimate—invasive, even—to be this close to the hem of her friend's skirt, but the tattoo calls to her. Almost voice-like, it speaks to her, tonality splitting into two distinct instruments. *A conversation.*

Darkness engulfs her, seeping from the periphery. She blinks the inky stains away to see a dimly lit room take shape around her. Two empty glasses of wine sit in front of her, translucent legs seeping down the sides of the glass—*still fresh.*

A low *pop* reaches her ears. She turns, following the sound.

"Kathleen isn't sleeping. Ever since… I just wish I knew how to help her." Michael's voice precedes him as he steps into view, a bottle of wine in hand. He offers

a sheepish smile. *"Or knew the first thing about what's going on in that head of hers."*

He talks about Kathleen like she isn't right here. *Why?*

"Baby Blue must have felt like a second chance," she says—voice distant, garbled, like she's underwater. *"It doesn't make sense why this keeps happening. And it's not her fault, of course. It's just anatomy. Or biology. I don't know. I flunked both of those classes. How does— how does this all feel for you?"*

Michael grunts softly, watching the wine churn in the glasses as he pours. *"Feels like a cruel twist of fate. Not to be overdramatic."*

She smiles, fondness blooming around her heart. *"You, overdramatic?"*

He chuckles. *"Me, overdramatic."*

"You know I'm here for you, right? For both of you."

He takes a sip. *"Has she talked to you much?"*

She shakes her head. *"No, but that doesn't mean she won't. She just needs some time, you know? So I'm helping how I can in the meantime, which means checking up on you."* She punctuates the last word with a poke to Michael's hand. Her fingers don't look like her own.

"Thank you." His smile is so fragile it nearly breaks Kathleen's heart. She knew that the miscarriages affected him too, but he always put on a brave face for her. *For both of them.*

"Of course." There's a pause before she asks, seemingly out of nowhere, *"Do you think you'll try again?"*

Michael blinks down at his glass. *"I'm not sure I want to. If it's going to have the same outcome, I just... I don't know if we could survive it."*

He's never said anything like that to her before. *Not even remotely.* How could she forget a conversation like this, odd and detached as it feels?

"Have you talked about it with her?"

He shakes his head, Adam's apple bobbing as he swallows back emotions. When he finally speaks, his voice sounds like a child's. *"I can't."*

"Why not?"

"It's all she wants. She wants to have a family."

"You two are a family. You don't need a child to be a family."

He stares up at the ceiling, stymieing tears. *"I don't know if I'm enough."*

"Michael," she says, scooting her chair closer until their knees are only centimeters apart. *"You're enough. You're more than enough. You're… You're the most incredible husband. She's so lucky—you're both so lucky to have found each other. There are so many men who wouldn't stick this kind of thing out. Who couldn't. They aren't wired for it. But you are. You've lived through it twice now. Whether you and Katy decide to try again, however that goes, you did the best you could. In my eyes, you are the best."*

Michael presses his fingers to his eyes, wiping tears away. Kathleen reaches for his other hand, balled up on his knee, squeezing. Before she can let go, he knots his fingers with hers. It's surreal, experiencing this profound moment, completely lost to her memory. *Completely foreign.*

What's stranger is how he lifts their hands to rest on her knee. What's even stranger than that is the feeling of his thumb rubbing the bare, sensitive skin of her thigh, goose bumps piling. Kathleen follows the feeling, staring down at her knee—no, not her knee. *Someone else's.*

"Diana," he murmurs, voice like an open wound—

"Katy?"

Kathleen hurls out of the moment and back to the office. She blinks up at her friend from her sprawl on the carpet, shuttled there and back in what must have only been a few seconds.

"Why are you on the floor?" Her friend yawns.

"It fell," she says, numbly lifting her hand. The ruby stud glitters pink against her palm.

"Oh," Diana says, eyes widening as she touches her ear. "It must have fallen out. Sorry, it's been hard to sleep at home without my girls there. Every dang creak wakes me up."

Kathleen rises to her feet, brushing dust from her pants. "Are you dreaming a lot?"

She thinks about it. "Not really. If I am, I never remember anything."

"What about memories? Ever since the Dreaming, has your, uh, memory improved?"

Diana's brows furrow. "What do you mean?"

"Like, reliving the past. Anything like that?"

"No. I mean, I'd kill to remember what hot food tastes like. It doesn't matter if it's a steaming forkful of chili peppers dunked in hot sauce—the moment it touches my tongue, ice cold. Feels like I'm living in some *would you rather* universe except I'd literally prefer any other torture than this. God, I have to pee so bad."

Diana stands and stretches, the run in her tights disappearing beneath the hem of her skirt. The memory— *Diana's memory*—is tucked away from Kathleen's prying eyes. The details are already fuzzy, and Kathleen strains to remember the scene she just witnessed. The little she saw of it must have taken place at Diana's house, only a few blocks away from her own.

Why was Michael touching Diana like that? Why was he looking at Diana like that?

She's bursting with questions, but she can't very well follow her friend into the bathroom. Before Diana can reach the door, a half-baked plan forms.

"Why don't you come over for dinner tonight?" she blurts. "We can experiment with the whole temperature thing and see if there's a workaround. Everyone deserves a hot meal, especially you, oh mother of three."

She internally winces for laying it on too thick. But Diana only smiles.

"You know, that would be so nice. I'd love that. Thank you, Katy. I can bring a casserole? The kind that can be eaten hot *or* cold," she says, her wry smile disappearing into the hall.

"Sounds perfect!" Kathleen calls after her.

A door closes down the hall, and Kathleen slumps into the chair. She reaches for her cell, thumb hovering over Michael's name.

She could just ask him. She could give him the chance to explain what she saw.

It's probably nothing.

Still, her friend's voice echoes in her ears.

"You're… You're the most incredible husband. She's so lucky—you're both so lucky to have found each other…"

No, she doesn't want to bring Michael into this. She needs to get Diana alone. She needs to know what happened that night between her husband and her best friend. Even if it's nothing at all, something has sparked inside of Kathleen, her every insecurity fanning the flame. The only way to stop it from burning through her from the inside out is to see the truth for herself.

All of it.

Chapter 11

At home, Kathleen catches up on the elder Wisemans.

"Mom is more or less the same," Michael says, standing over the kitchen counter's spread of ingredients. "Her ears are pointed like Mary's. She's planning on growing her hair out to hide them. I told her she doesn't have to, but you know…"

"What about Duke?"

The knife in his hand slows against the cutting board. "He's, uh, different. Lost all his hair, plus about a foot of height. At least that's what Mom told me. He wouldn't let me see him. He's totally isolated himself."

Sitting at the table, Kathleen sets down the potato peeler in her hands to look up at Michael. The line of his shoulders seems so fragile. *Ever since Travis.*

"He just needs time," she says, but her consolations sound empty to her own ears.

Michael doesn't seem to notice, throwing her a smile. "Probably. It'll be nice to have Diana over tonight. She's a good distraction."

Dread drops like an anchor in Kathleen's gut. *She's a good distraction.* How often has Diana been a good distraction to her husband? Her tongue itches with the question.

"She needs a distraction of her own these days," she says instead, focusing back on the task at hand. "With Eric taking the girls full-time, she's a complete wreck. I haven't been a very good friend to her lately."

"You're a great friend," he rebuts, wiping his hands on a dish towel. "And Diana is a grown woman. She can take care of herself."

"Maybe."

Leaning against the sink, Michael watches her work. He looks so good in their natural habitat—towel slung over his shoulder, half a smile on his lips, blond hair catching the final rays of sunset. He's a fixture of her home, her kitchen, her heart. It breaks her.

I love you. I love you. I love you. I love you. I love—

"It's good of you to invite her over," he says. "We have to band together during times like these. We can't isolate. There's too much grief to hold alone. We have to be there for each other."

Wine-laced words come to mind. *"You know I'm here for you, right? For both of you."*

The peeler slips in Kathleen's hands, slicing her fingertip. Before she can even react, he's kneeling before her, examining the cut with a furrowed brow.

"Ouch," he commiserates. "Hold on, I'll get the first-aid kit."

"It's okay. I'll go clean up."

"You sure? I can—"

"Really, it's fine. Thank you." She drops a quick kiss to the top of his head as she stands. It's reflexive, and it carves a new emptiness for her malaise to fill.

Under the bathroom lights, the cut looks and bleeds like a raw beet. Kathleen wonders if her heart looks just as angry as this wound. Bracing against the sink, she takes a shuddering breath. It'll be a long night if she can't keep her cool. With confrontation on the horizon, she needs to be ready to handle herself. She can't fall apart.

Just as she secures the bandage around her finger, a car beeps outside. *She's here.*

"I'll get it," Kathleen calls down the stairs. At the door, the breath she's been holding fizzles out on a puzzled sigh. Diana is paused on the sidewalk with none other than Nadine Jones—backpack slung over her shoulder, signature camera case hanging around her neck. She still wears a hoodie, but this time her canary yellow hair is tied up in a messy bun.

Good, Kathleen thinks. *She shouldn't hide.*

"Oh, Haley will be so thrilled," Diana is saying. "Why don't you give me your number? We can set up a time for next week."

Nadine recites her number, glancing at Kathleen on the porch. Her once hazel eyes are now a bright amber, almost as golden as the setting sun.

"Kathleen! Nadine is going to tutor Haley!" Diana announces. Under normal circumstances, her smile would be contagious. "Only as often as she has time for, of course. It's the end of senior year, after all. You've gotta make the most of it!"

Nadine's smile looks more like a grimace. "Well, I'll probably be around your place a lot, since the hospital is that way."

Diana claps a hand over her heart. "That's right. I heard about your friend… Jackie? How is she doing? There was some kind of accident, right?"

"*Jax* is in a coma," Nadine quietly corrects. "But the doctors think he'll wake up any day now. I'm trying to visit every day after school until he does."

Diana nods, her mouth opening and closing like a fish's.

"We'll be thinking about him," Kathleen offers, taking the social cue from the youngest among them. Kathleen can't imagine going through any of this as a teenager. "And you."

"Thanks," Nadine whispers, dropping her gaze to the sidewalk as her brave face falters. "I better get going. I've got homework to do."

Diana miraculously finds her voice again. "Of course, sweetie. Do you want a ride?"

"I'm just down the block," Nadine calls over her shoulder, pulling her hood over her head. "I'll be alright! Thank you."

Muttering, Diana shuffles to the passenger side to retrieve her infamous casserole. Kathleen watches Nadine's shrinking silhouette, empathy she didn't know she had left tugging at her heart. When she raises a hand to block what's left of the sun's dying rays, she sees it—a smudge, just like she saw at Travis's grave. It follows Nadine from a few paces behind, too big to be like Hilary's tail but too singular to be a vestige of the setting sun.

A trick of the light?

"That girl worries me," Diana is saying. "Maybe it's just all my maternal instincts looking for somewhere to go. She seems like a fraction of herself these days."

"I didn't know that a high schooler was hospitalized. Because of the Dreaming?"

Diana shakes her head. "I don't know the specifics. I think there was an accident of some kind. I wanted to ask but… Who knew Jackie Clark is *Jax* Clark now?" A pout forms on her lips. "I'm useless on my own. My girls keep me young."

"Come on inside," Kathleen says, her hand automatically reaching to pat her friend's back. She drops it awkwardly to her side, earning an odd look from Diana.

"What's up?"

"Not a lot. Why?" She avoids her friend's gaze, locking the door behind them.

"Just—are you okay? You seem a little off," Diana whispers. *So Michael doesn't hear.*

"We're all a little off these days. It's part of the territory. Did you change your jewelry?"

Diana pulls a strand of loose hair from her dangling earrings. "Yeah, I must have lost the backing on that stud. It didn't match the outfit anyway."

She had clearly changed after work. Gone are the ripped tights, replaced now with a pair of high-waisted jeans. *All covered up.* As before, her torso is swathed in a thick-knit sweater, this time a complimentary lavender. Her head and hands are all that's left for prying eyes—*my eyes.*

"I like your hair like this," Kathleen says. "The braid is nice." *Just act normal.*

Diana smiles, those blue eyes fixed to the floor. She seems fifteen years younger in one simple gesture. "Thanks, Katy. I thought, well, you're not hiding it. So why should I?"

In the kitchen, Michael is loading their dinner into the oven. It smells like garlic, butter, and nostalgia. It makes Kathleen wish she had a drink in her hands.

"Welcome in," he says. "What have you got there?"

"Just a casserole. It's all I'm good for these days. Is there room for it in the oven? It'll just need about fifteen minutes at three-fifty."

"Well, let's see here. We can play a little *Tetris*…"

Kathleen lingers in the doorway, watching her best friend and her husband putter around the stove together, acting so domestic. *Like a couple.*

"Does anyone want some wine?" she asks, already reaching for the rack. The first bottle her fingers touch is a pinot noir. She tasted a jammy red on Diana's tongue that fateful night.

Seems only right.

"I'll take a splash," Diana says as Michael pulls three glasses from the cabinets.

Kathleen passes him the bottle. "Do you like Diana's hair?"

He grins, excruciatingly normal. "It looks great. The color suits you."

Diana scoffs. "I still look like a Smurf."

"Smurfs have yellow hair, if they have hair at all," Michael playfully corrects.

"Did you see Nadine's, Katy? It's *so* yellow."

The sound of cork on glass makes Kathleen flinch.

"I just wish I knew how to help her," he said that night, uncorked bottle in hand. *"Or knew the first thing about what's going on in that head of hers."*

"I just wonder what's going on in that head of hers," Kathleen echoes, eyes trained on her husband's malleable expression.

He only nods, pouring heavily into the glasses. "Administration has their hands full lately. Every time I call, I'm put on hold for a minimum of twenty minutes. I think I know that music by heart now." He sings it softly, badly—prompting a giggle from Diana.

Kathleen takes a long swig of wine. Yes, this was the flavor on Diana's tongue when she said, *"It's just anatomy. Or biology. I don't know. I flunked both of those classes."*

"What is Nadine going to tutor Haley in, Diana? Anatomy? Biology?"

"Oh, Haley loves science. It's English that's the problem," Diana says. "She's the most left-brained of us all, but high school teachers won't be so lenient on grammar and spelling."

"You said they could start next week. Do you think you'll have the girls back by then?"

"I did say that, didn't I?" Diana sighs heavily. "I guess that was just my subconscious speaking. Sorry, we don't have to get into this. I don't want to cry before dinner."

"You can cry all over our dinner for all we care," Michael says in his frustratingly gentle way. "Your girls will be back before you know it. The more we learn about the Dreaming, the more we'll be able to protect the ones that matter to us most. It's just a matter of time. In the meantime, your friends are here for you while you wait this one out."

Diana swipes at a stray tear with the back of her hand. "Feels like forever."

"Feels like a cruel twist of fate. Not to be overdramatic."

"You, overdramatic?"

"Me, overdramatic."

Kathleen knocks her glass off the table and right into Diana's lap.

"I'm so sorry." She gasps. "My hand slipped and—oh, it's everywhere…"

"Here," Michael says, dutifully offering paper towels.

"If you don't wash it out, it'll stain. I'm sure I have something you can change into."

"No, no, it's okay." Diana laughs, unbothered. "Just fill her glass again!"

"I insist," Kathleen says, pulling her friend toward the stairs. "We've got time, right?"

Michael glances at the timer. "About ten minutes and maybe an extra five to cool."

"Perfect."

Diana follows Kathleen up the stairs, grumbling as she goes. "You're delusional if you think any of your clothes will fit me."

Kathleen shoos her into the bathroom regardless. "Just let me see what I've got."

"For wine, is it hot or cold water you're supposed to rinse with?" Diana projects through the cracked door, loud enough to reach the bedroom.

But Kathleen lingers in the hall, listening to Diana shuffle out of her jeans and turn the faucet on. Carefully, quietly, she presses her palm to the door, staring at her scarlet skin, willing a story she knows like the back of her hand to form exactly there.

Come on, she begs of her strange abilities. *I need to see what happened.*

"Katy?" her friend calls again.

A shape flickers across her knuckles, shimmering. *There.*

Kathleen presses the door open, meeting Diana's surprised eyes in the mirror.

"Find something already?" she asks.

Hands empty, Kathleen drops her eyes to her friend's bare leg. Dark tendrils coil around Diana's thigh as darkness creeps around the edges of Kathleen's vision.

It's working.

"Katy?"

What follows the black isn't so much a vision as it is a feeling—a pressure on her mouth. She feels a hot puff of air slip between her lips... a sigh.

A kiss.

Kathleen's eyes—*Diana's eyes*—flutter open to see a familiar fan of blond eyelashes above a smattering of pale freckles. *Michael's freckles.* He's kissing her. It's a familiar sensation to Kathleen, but through Diana, it feels as intoxicating as the wine on their lips. She angles her mouth against his, breathing him in. He smells like home. His hand on her thigh feels like freedom.

Kathleen can't take another second. Scrunching her eyes closed, she wills the moment to pass. She has all the information she needs, but the memories have other plans.

When she opens her eyes, it's not to her upstairs bathroom, but to the alley behind the shop. It's warm outside—*summertime*. Her eyes focus on a jewelry box held open in two familiar hands, two familiar studs glimmering in the sunlight.

Rubies.

"These are for you," Micheal says. *"Happy birthday."*

"I can't take these."

"Of course you can," he insists. *"You don't have to wear them if you don't like them."*

"No, they're beautiful," she murmurs, clasping the box tightly in her hands. *"Thank you. Don't you and Katy share accounts though? How did you…"*

"I had Travis make them off the record. Told him they were for my mother." His posture sinks a bit, his guilt weighing on them both.

"We can't do this anymore," she whispers, eyes darting toward the door.

"I know we can't. Don't you think I know that? But I can't ignore my feelings for you."

"You can, and we have to," Diana insists. *"No matter how we feel about each other, we have a responsibility to Kathleen. She's finally opening up again,*

and now is the time to prove to her that you're on her side. We have to be there for her. We can't keep lying like this. I can't."

Michael drops his arms from her shoulders, taking a step back. *"You told Eric."*

Hot tears pool in her eyes. *"No, I didn't. He's suspicious though. I think he knows."*

"How could he? We've been so careful."

"Michael, I'm pregnant."

Michael blinks at her, stunned. *"You are? Who...?"*

Kathleen has never seen so many emotions cross her husband's face at once—fear, hope, *love.* It makes her sick to her stomach. Just as she feels the impulse to press her hands to her belly, Diana does exactly that. *Where a baby would be.*

"I don't know who the father is."

Kathleen closes her eyes. *No.*

The warmth of a foreign hand on her belly coaxes her into the next memory. But the hand isn't foreign at all—it's her own. She's watching herself, Kathleen Wiseman, feel the baby kick under her best friend's woolen sweater. Diana must be seven or eight months along here. Kathleen feels an alien presence shift in her belly, haunted and fascinated in equal measure.

"She's a kicker." Diana sighs.

"Wow, she really is. Have you landed on any names?" the-Kathleen-of-then asks, genuine awe on her face. Kathleen-of-now wants to smack her.

"Not yet," Diana whispers. *"Haley's and Julia's names came to me so fast. This little one... I'm not so sure. I think we'll wait to meet her before we give her a name."*

"Three sisters." Her past self sighs. *"They're so lucky to have you as a mom."*

A painful lump lodges in Diana's throat. Kathleen can feel her remorse, her thick-as-tar guilt piling behind her tongue as she fights the impulse to spill the truth and tell her everything.

Instead, she says, *"They're luckier to have you as the coolest aunt in town."*

"And godmother." The naive pride in her own voice makes Kathleen furious, nausea turning over into a steady boil.

How could I be this stupid?

When she blinks, that boil erupts into unbearable pain—fire burning through her belly, hips, and pelvis. Through her hot tears, fluorescent lights create colorful floaters in her field of vision. A woman screams through gasping breaths, throat tearing with sheer volume.

It's Diana. *Diana is screaming.*

"In, in, out," a man coaches. *"In through the nose, out through the mouth. Come on, Diana, you've got this. In, in, out..."*

In her delirium, she recognizes Eric's face hovering over her. He winces as she squeezes his hand, feeling the muscle and bone fight against her iron grip.

"Hee, hee, hoooo..." She wheezes.

Diana is giving birth. This is the third time, and it isn't any easier. For Kathleen, however, it's the very first time. It *hurts*. It hurts like nothing she's ever experienced, muscles stretched and pulled to their limits while her organs contract, forcing life into the world.

It's what she's always wanted, and simultaneously, it's enough to ruin her.

The tears on her cheeks feel like her own when a piercing, hiccupping wail rips through the room—*the baby's first cry.*

It's over. Eric's face beams over her as her eyes close from utter exhaustion. Kathleen is so light, she could just float away…

Instead, Kathleen opens her eyes to another room—another memory. A rocking chair creaks softly in a nursery, decorated floor to ceiling with painted flowers and glow-in-the-dark stars. Kathleen remembers standing on a chair when Diana was pregnant with Haley, pressing those very stars into their constellations.

Something shifts in her arms. There, the most precious creature sleeps, tightly swaddled so only her little pink face pokes through the cotton.

Michaela.

With those blonde eyelashes, how could she have named her anything else?

Diana sighs contentedly while Kathleen reels. She feels insane with rage. She could laugh. It was so obvious—in front of her face this whole time.

"Diana," comes a voice from the doorway. Eric stands there, a rolling suitcase at his feet and a piece of paper in his hands.

"What's wrong?" Diana whispers. *"Do you have to go back to work?"*

He sighs, rubbing his eyes with the back of his hand. They're red, like he's been crying.

"I may not be the brightest," he mumbles, holding the paper aloft, *"but I'm smart enough to know that someone who has type AB blood can't have a daughter with type O."*

"Eric…"

The room goes dark around Kathleen, sucking her from the nursery to the upstairs bathroom of Kathleen's house. *The present.* The smell hits her before she sees the smoke. As she stands at the bathroom door, her hand glows bright hot, hissing against the wood. Diana stands before her, mouth agape as she stares at the embers between Kathleen's fingertips.

"Katy?" she repeats, this time with urgency. "There's—your hand—fire!"

Slowly, Kathleen removes her hand, staring at the perfectly scorched impression stained on the wood. Her bandage has completely burnt away. When her eyes flicker back to Diana's, she can feel the heat of her glare roll off her in waves. When she speaks, her voice crackles like flames.

"Were you ever going to tell me?"

Chapter 12

Diana's dumbstruck expression only feeds Kathleen's fury. The woman she once called her best friend scrambles back into her wine-stained jeans.

"You're burning," she squeaks, terrified. "Oh my god, we—we have to get Mi—"

"You don't get to see Michael. Not now, not ever again."

Kathleen hardly recognizes herself. She's never sounded this clear to her own ears. She likes it. She likes how the rage sits on her shoulders, like a mantle she was born to wear.

"Answer the question."

"What are you talking about? I don't know what you're saying!"

"When were you going to tell me that you slept with Michael?"

Diana gets paler by the second. "Katy…"

"What's going on?" Michael calls from below. His curiosity turns wide-eyed when he reaches the bottom of the stairs. "Oh my god, Kathleen! Your hand—"

"Yes, fire!" Diana urges. "Get the extinguish—"

"*No!*" Kathleen screams, voice tearing through them all. "Don't speak to him! No one moves until I get the truth!"

Silence percolates around them, save for the soft hiss of flames licking up Kathleen's wrists. Their whisper is a comfort. *Power is a comfort.*

"When did it happen?"

The two exchange a look, their nonanswer almost as damning as an explanation.

Michael takes a sharp breath, his words measured. "What are we talking about?"

Kathleen whips around, pointing at him with an accusing finger. "You *know!*"

No one expects the flare that leaps from her pointed finger, shooting like a bullet toward Michael's head. At the last second, he dodges, falling against the banister as the fireball rockets through the front door instead—a wreath-shaped hole left in its wake.

"*Kathleen!*" Diana screams, reaching for her shoulder to yank the burning woman back. A plume of steam rises between them at the contact. Before she knows for sure what's happening, Diana is pushing past her to rush down the stairs.

"I didn't mean… ," Kathleen tries, her throat dry.

Diana pulls Michael to his feet. "Are you hurt?"

Dazed, he stares unblinkingly at Kathleen. "I'm fine."

Her grip on his arm is too familiar. Kathleen's guilt evaporates just like that. Jealousy is the accelerator for the fire racing up her arms to set her hair ablaze. Step by step, she descends the stairs, embers chewing through the wood like hellbound termites.

"Don't *touch* him," Kathleen growls. "Don't you *dare* touch each other."

They jump back from each other, mirroring their horror.

"Katy, you have to breathe," Diana pleads, hands open "You have to cool off. You're burning the house down and us with it.

"It was a mistake," Michael begins to cry, tears racing past his freckled cheeks. "It was wrong, and we're so sorry. We failed you. We know that."

"We, we, we," Kathleen mutters. "When did you two become a *we*? When did you decide that fucking was the best option? After my second miscarriage? My third?"

The wood of the banister splits against the furnace of Kathleen's grip. It feels incredible, this righteous pain. It sings through her like it belongs to a higher power and she's merely the vessel for its divine will.

"Did you think naming her Michaela was cute?" she spits. "Gosh, you must have shared a laugh at my expense. Eric knew, didn't he? He told me to stop fighting your battles for you. I didn't understand what he meant. I guess I was the last to know. I can't believe how stupid I've been." Her eyes flit from Diana to Michael, scathing. "Where did it happen? How many times? In our bed? In our shop?"

Michael's face contorts with shame.

"It was a few times," Diana blurts. "We were looking for comfort in all the wrong places. Eric and I were fighting all the time, and I should have been focusing on the girls—Michael should have been focusing on you—"

"I'm so sorry, Kathleen," he repeats. "I never wanted to hurt you."

"Then why hurt me? Why cheat on me with my best friend? How could you? How could either of you? I don't—I don't understand—" Kathleen can feel her grip on her rage slipping. Tears sizzle against her cheeks, stinging like acid. "I can't *begin* to understand!"

"I love you," Michael pleads. "It's you and me, Kathleen. It's always been you and me."

Beneath the screech of the fire alarm, the oven beeps. *Dinner is ready*. She wants to break something—to break it and break it some more until the ruin on the inside becomes ruin on the outside. With a howl, Kathleen storms past Diana and Michael, the two cowering against the coatrack like cornered animals. In the kitchen, she rips the oven open, grabbing the dishes inside with bare hands. They feel like nothing against her skin—not hot, not cold, just mass.

"No one's ever getting between my Katy and me," Diana once promised.

On my wedding day.

Raising the casserole above her head, she slams it to the floor. Glass shatters and food splatters every which way. It's not enough. Nothing is enough to feed this appetite for destruction.

By the time Michael ducks into the room, she's breaking every dish in the sink.

"Go!" Kathleen screams, the window rattling. "Go away!"

"I'm not going anywhere." He's never sounded more scared.

"You had a baby with her," she wails. "You have a child with her."

Kathleen tenses as she's jerked back by two arms—the familiar weight of her husband's embrace like a straitjacket filled with fire ants.

"Let me go," she sobs.

"No. You're my family, Kathleen. You're my family."

He turns her around, wrapping her tightly in his arms. She's a pressure cooker, moments from capacity. There's movement in her peripheral as Diana steps into view, tears rolling down her round cheeks.

"Let her go, Michael," she demands. "It's all out there now, right? We all know I'm the one who wedged myself into your lives and ruined everything. It was all me. I wanted what you had, Katy, and I took it for myself."

"You know that's not what happened," Michael argues, but it's too late. Kathleen is already firing another blast at Diana's head.

The woman tears out the front door. *Running away.*

Kathleen won't let her. She wrestles free from Michael's arms to give chase. The front door is decimated now, just splinters hanging from the hinges. As Diana scrambles down the steps, Kathleen sends another hail of fire. It misses, carving a hole out of their porch railing, but that's no matter. The fire comes at no cost to Kathleen, reaching so deep within her that it connects to something primal—an instinctual power.

My power.

My fire.

Seeing the fear in Diana's eyes, Kathleen finally understands. The Dreaming didn't give her the ability to tap into some higher power. It just unlocked her true potential. The Dreaming gave her back her rage.

The blast from a fireball sweeps Diana off her feet, tossing her to the ground like a rag doll. Thrusting both hands out, Kathleen channels a wall of white-hot fury at Diana, whose face contorts into a banshee-like wail—a final plea.

"Katy, please! STOP!"

What happens next transpires in the span of a blink.

The bright fire reflects across Diana's glassy face before she disappears behind a jagged sheet of ice, like an elemental force field.

The scream crescendos to a fever pitch, as if the atoms themselves are crying.

Then, the collision—a blast that's hotter than hot. Louder than anything Kathleen has ever heard.

Blinding light.

Utter silence.

Perfect, unfolding darkness.

* * *

When Kathleen opens her eyes again, she can't tell the stars from the sparks. Pushing up onto her elbows, she tries to reorient herself. Under her lay the splintered remains of her living room doors—the wall that separated the kitchen from the hearth obliterated. Now, the bones burn around her.

She doesn't realize her ears are ringing until she can barely hear the inflection of her own muffled name. Squinting through the ash and embers, she sees Diana. The woman closes in on her, arms wrapping around Kathleen's shoulders.

"Where's Michael?" Kathleen asks, her voice distant to her own ears.

"I don't know," Diana says, or at least Kathleen thinks she does.

"What happened?" *I can't remember.*

"There… as… n… plosion."

"What?"

"Explosion," Diana emphasizes, taking her face between two hands. *"Are you okay?"*

"I think so. Where's Micheal?" she asks again.

Keeping one hand on Kathleen's cheek, Diana sits up tall on her knees, squinting through the ash. There's red on her pants.

"You're bleeding."

"*—just wine,*" Diana assures her. *"—walk?" Wine? Walk where?*

She can hear the sirens now, her ears coming back to her. Soon, red lights reflect off her friend's pale face. Suddenly, she remembers how the fire reflected from her face too—*my fire.*

Kathleen grips Diana's wrist. *Did I do this?*

"Can you walk?" Diana asks again, voice clearer now.

She nods, letting Diana help her to her feet. Together, they hobble over bricks and bubbled plaster toward the minivan. The sliding door is concave now, a human-sized dent folded into the metal. Surrounded by broken glass, a man lays in a twisted heap in their driveway. She can't see his face beneath the burns.

Kathleen's knees buckle from under her. Stomach churning, she crawls after Diana, gripping palmfuls of grass for leverage while her friend takes the man's hand between her own.

"Wake up," she is begging. "Kathleen's right here. She's coming…"

Kathleen's field of vision fills with thick black galoshes. *The firefighters are here.*

"Ma'am," one says, "are you in any pain? Are you injured?"

"I'm okay," she insists, but her head spins when she tries to stand. Two sets of hands steady her, gently guiding her back to the ground.

"Don't move," another instructs. "Can you tell us what happened here?"

"An explosion..."

All around her, responders rush as close as they can to the still burning house, pulling a hose from the fire engine. The whole Thistle Grove fire department must be here.

It must have been a big explosion, Kathleen muses. She can hardly remember.

Diana shuffles uselessly behind a team of paramedics. Kathleen doesn't notice the heavy woolen blanket around her shoulders until it falls to the ground as she stands to follow her.

"Where's Micheal?" she asks again.

Glassy-eyed, Diana stares at the ambulance doors closing. "We should follow them."

Without knowing why, she's being directed into Diana's minivan. All hands on deck to quell the flames, there's no one to stop them from getting into the van and pulling through Randall's yard onto the street. Diana follows close behind the ambulance, one hand on the wheel and the other on Kathleen's wrist, gripping tight. Diana's thumb rubs a clean spot from the soot on the back of Kathleen's hand in an effort to comfort her.

Or herself.

The whole drive, she coaches Kathleen on their story.

"People are going to ask questions. We're going to tell them it was a freak accident," she says, the tremor in her voice hardly contained by her firm tone. "We were sitting down to dinner when Michael realized he'd left the oven on. Next thing we knew, the house was up in flames..."

When they pull into the ER bay, a team of four are unloading a battered and bloodied man from the ambulance. Kathleen stumbles from the van, steadying herself on the hood as she staggers closer. Poking out from the edges of a head bandage is a shock of blond hair. One of the stretcher wheels skids on a bump, and a dappled black and red hand hangs limply off the edge—a white-gold wedding band on his finger.

Michael.

"Can you see him?" Diana asks just as she cracks open the driver's side door.

Kathleen spins around to slam it shut, stabilizing herself with one hand on the roof, the other on the handle. Confused, Diana attempts to open it again, and Kathleen shoves her whole body weight against the car. Her own words echo like a mantra in her mind.

You don't get to see Michael. Not now, not ever again.

Not now, not ever again.

Not ever again.

Kathleen's anger is back, weaker than before but still hot enough to melt metal. She focuses it all on the handle, welding it into place as she stares into her friend's teary eyes. The door doesn't budge as she yanks from the inside.

"Go home," she commands. "Go home, Diana."

When she turns to follow the team into the vestibule, Kathleen doesn't look back.

After offering all necessary identification, she sits in the waiting area for who knows how long. Staring down at her hands, she imagines that their hue is only the product of red and black pastels. *Not some supernatural event.* Has no time passed since she was only a little girl on a hospital bench, waiting to hear whether her parents would survive the night?

She doesn't remember calling Patricia, but she'd recognize that voice anywhere.

"Where is he?" his mother demands, grabbing a nurse by the arm. She must have been notified by the staff. That or news simply travels that fast in a town this small.

Kathleen strains to hear the nurse's response, too low for her ears to catch. Patricia's wail could break glass. Heaving to her feet, she approaches with uneven steps.

"Is he okay?" Kathleen asks, her voice hoarse from all the screaming.

She's seen that very look on a nurse's face once before, many years ago.

"Demon!" Patricia wails, pointing at Kathleen. "You're a *demon*! You stole my son from me, you devil! You killed him! You did this! You did this! You did this…"

Chapter 13

A knock at the front door wakes Kathleen from a restless sleep. Eyes still closed, she reaches across the pillow, feeling nothing but cotton.

Is he making breakfast?

But no sounds filter from the floor below, and the only smells that reach her nose are must and ammonia.

The knock comes again, this time louder—closer.

Kathleen's eyes creak open like two ancient doors, but not to a familiar sight. It's dark in this room, no open window cloaked in silvery, embroidered curtains to sway in the breeze. Instead, Kathleen recognizes the heavy drapes of a hotel room.

Oh.

That's right. After she gave her statement to the police at the hospital, Kathleen checked herself into a hotel. She reserved the room indefinitely, stripped out of her smoke-logged clothes the moment the door closed behind her, and collapsed atop the quilted comforter. Prior to last night, she'd never stayed at this hotel, the only one in Thistle Grove. Prior to last night, she'd had a bed of her own to sleep in. *To share.*

This she knows for sure—gone are the days where Kathleen would wake up and know exactly where she is.

The hotel concierge standing at her door is short, round, and avian. He looks like a porch goose in a button-up with two downy wings folded neatly down his sides.

"Sorry to wake you, miss," he says with remarkable clarity through a flat bill. "Someone dropped this off for you."

He rolls a large suitcase forward until it bumps the threshold.

She recognizes the magenta color but asks nevertheless, "Who was it?"

He shrugs, already waddling back down the hall. "No name. Some blue lady."

For the next two days, she leaves the suitcase in the hall until she can't stand the smell of smoke on her clothes for another miserable second. Dragging the bag inside, Kathleen heaves it onto the luggage rack with a huff. She crouches low, pulling the zipper like a trained technician might disarm a bomb. It doesn't explode, though, merely revealing a variety of new clothes and toiletries.

She didn't even leave a note. It's a relief, honestly.

Kathleen slips into a gray crew neck sweater and a pair of black leggings before venturing outside for the first time in days. Her hair is still wet from the shower, and the spring breeze wakes her up with its cooling touch. Earlier that morning, the police called to say that the report had been filed and she was welcome to salvage whatever remains of her home.

The walk is long, spanning from one end of town to the other. Her hands feel oddly empty—no wallet, keys, or phone as auxiliary limbs. Just her hotel key card pokes out of her leggings pocket. She feels particularly naked without her phone, the very technology that kept her in touch with the Dreaming before she knew what it was. Without it, Kathleen is forced to keep her head up, taking in Thistle Grove like it's the very first time. The streets are largely bare, with most townsfolk at work or school, and Kathleen is grateful to avoid unwanted stares. It isn't until she reaches her own block that the rumor mill catches up to her.

"… gone to hell in a handbasket," an older lady with a lopsided wig is saying to a taller woman. Kathleen recognizes them as the elderly sisters who walk the neighborhood every day, often stopping to whisper about *so-and-so's* garden and *this-and-that* botched renovation. Now, they stand before the ruins of her home, not bothering to lower their voices. "Thistle Grove just isn't what it used to be, is it?"

"Fires and break-ins." Her sister sighs. Two elven ears sprout from her perm. "It wasn't like this when we were growing up."

"What break-in?" Kathleen asks.

Both women jolt, whipping around to see Kathleen only a few paces away.

"There was a home invasion down the street a few nights ago," the elf scoffs, as if this were news Kathleen should have already known. "Same night as the horrible fire here."

"Whose home? Is everyone okay?"

"I don't think that the *Joneses* have anything to worry about," the wigged woman snarks. "They probably have insurance for whatever was stolen."

"I heard that Nadia girl was home when it happened," her sister adds.

Oh no…

"Nadine Jones?"

"How am I supposed to know?" she mutters, beckoning to the other. "Let's go…"

The wigged woman scurries after, whispering, "Isn't that the same woman who lived in that house? Patricia's daughter-in-law?"

While they take their gossip with them, Kathleen says a silent prayer for Nadine and her family. She doesn't pray to any god in particular, just to a higher power that might intercede on a child's behalf, even if it's ignored Kathleen's plight so far. It's all she can manage.

The Wiseman house looks like a war zone. A solitary wall leans haphazardly against a series of scorched beams, stooped piles of rubble where rooms once stood tall. It's impossible to imagine that this desolate scene was once a loving home. That makes it easier for Kathleen to rifle through the remains. Gone are the stairs, the French doors, and the hearth. The garage is decimated too—the car with it—so there's no point in looking for the keys. With the structure in utter ruins, their belongings stood no chance against the blaze. It's bizarre to think that she once had a closet full of clothes, that she once decided to save a dress for a nicer day, so certain that a nicer day would come.

Now, all of her dresses are ash.

With the rooms so unrecognizable from each other, she only knows she's found the kitchen when she steps over the melted frame of their old box television, its glass shattered into hundreds of tiny black shards.

Only a month ago, she sat down at the table with her husband and watched that fateful report from Wales.

Only days ago, Michael held her in his arms in this very room, begging for her forgiveness as hellfire careened from her fingertips.

Only hours ago, she might have convinced herself that he was still alive.

Later that afternoon, Kathleen sits at Madame Butterfried's with Michael's glasses held delicately between her soot-stained fingers. The lenses are gone, only a twisted mass of melted metal remaining. It was a miracle she found them at all. Everything else is unsalvageable—their creaky chairs, the coffee maker they should have retired years ago, the bed they shared…

Her rings are gone too. She's not sure when she lost them. *Probably melted away.*

"Here. Safe," she told Michael, presenting them from her pocket after she'd spent the night cleaning the fireplace.

"I'm listening," he promised, sliding them back onto her finger with a reverent kiss.

She hasn't cried yet. None of it feels real. Kathleen expects Michael to walk through the door every time the door chimes overhead. When someone sits across from her, she expects to be met with his contagious smile.

Instead, she's met with the empathetic eyes of the diner's owner.

"Can I get you something to eat, hun? Despite what they say, you can't live off coffee alone," Hilary says. "You want a nice plate of steak and eggs?"

Kathleen shakes her head. "Can I borrow your phone?"

"Sure thing," Hilary says, blinking back her surprise. She pulls it out of her apron pocket and hands it over right away. "Here. Password is Dillon's birthday. 72909."

Abrasive as the two elderly sisters may have been, they reminded her of an important task on her to-do list. She'll have to file an insurance claim. Kathleen takes Hilary's phone to the bathroom with her, Googling the number. After navigating the company's automated menu, she's connected with an agent. The conversation turns sour in record timing.

"Since the landscape has changed, accidents of that nature require special investigating," the agent explains. "If we deem that the accident was a result of *acute metamorphic oneirosis*, then unfortunately you are not covered by your current policy."

Acute metamorphic oneirosis—AMO. Kathleen remembers it as the Dreaming's more widely accepted name. Basic acts of God don't include magical outbursts, it seems.

"We weren't informed that we needed extra coverage."

"We sent notice out in the mail earlier this month," he says. "It would have been in your email too. According to our records, Michael Wiseman received an email outlining the importance of adding the new policy to your coverage twelve days ago. We asked our valued clients to purchase the policy by the end of the month."

"That was—" *Days ago.* "We didn't see anything come through the mail, and my husband barely checks his email. How do you expect people to adapt so quickly?"

"The world of accident insurance is one that must move quickly to reflect the times," he responds diplomatically, almost certainly reading from a script.

Kathleen massages her temple with her free hand. "So, what does it mean if the investigation deems that the house was destroyed due to, um, circumstances of *AMO*?"

"I'm afraid there's nothing we can do for you."

If it was her phone, Kathleen would have flung it against the tile wall. Instead, she hangs up on the agent and gently sets the phone on the sink's edge before crumpling to the ground. Staring at the layered footprints of diner regulars, it suddenly occurs to her that she'll never be barefoot in her own bathroom again. She'll never stand at the sink and brush her teeth alongside her person. She'll never see his reflection next to hers in the mirror.

Bile rushes up her throat before she can register its heat. She coughs up the acidic coffee into the toilet bowl, head pounding.

Kathleen has survived a lot. She lost her parents at a young age, raised herself under the neglectful glances of an absentee grandmother, and miraculously made it out of the foster care system with some of her dignity.

But on this day, in this diner bathroom, she's never felt more alone.

Chapter 14

It's a month before Kathleen is able to set foot in Jenkins' Jewelers. When she made the sale, she agreed to empty the place of all personal items. Joseph and Mary were kind enough to take on the bulk of the work, but today is the last day they'll have access. Today, she has to say goodbye.

Last week, Michael's parents filed a wrongful death suit against their daughter-in-law. Without an insurance payout, Kathleen can't afford the legal representation she needs to fight them. So, the shop had to go, and all her hard work with it. Secretly, she doesn't think she'll win. She's resigned herself to a world in which every reminder of her old life will be cruelly and systematically stripped from her.

Even now, her livelihood sits in boxes around her—a sad reminder of how easy it is to pack up a life with some cardboard and tape. All stock has been relocated to the vault for safekeeping until the new owners move in and make Jenkins' Jewelers their own.

I wonder what they'll call it.

Reaching under the cash register, Kathleen finds the small notebook where she'd scribbled down all the potential names for their business. *Useless now.*

Still, she reads.

Wiseman Wares/Wears?
MK Jewelers
Wisteria Jewelers
Whimsy and Wiseman

"Likewise Jewelers," she whispers aloud, remembering Diana's last suggestion before everything came to light. *Before I burned it all down.*

She hasn't seen Diana in a month. She hasn't disappeared or anything—small reminders of her existence litter Kathleen's life on a daily basis. Food showing up at her hotel door that she didn't order, gift cards arriving in her P.O. box, missed calls from the same local number on her new phone… Kathleen can only hope that Diana will stop assuaging her own guilt if she ignores her long enough.

The paper rips easily in her hands. Page after page, she tears the notebook to pieces.

A clatter from the workshop drags her from her reverie.

"All good!" Joseph calls. "Just knocked over the stool with this ridiculous tail of mine."

"*Magnificent* tail, you mean," his wife clarifies, emerging from the office. She gingerly steps over the paper scraps. Pausing over one in particular, Mary glances curiously at its contents before plucking it from the ground. "You might want to keep this one."

"What one?" Her tone is harsher than it needs to be, but Mary is unfazed. She holds it out to Kathleen with a small knowing smile.

"This one."

Kathleen takes the page, and her heart nearly stops cold when she recognizes the handwriting—
Michael's.

It's written in his crisp, somewhat lopsided lettering.

Another candidate: Aelwyd Jewelers.
Aelwyd means "hearth" in Welsh. It's stuck with me since we visited. I think because it reminds me of you.

— M

Kathleen swipes at the tear rolling down her cheek before it drops onto the page. Tears have never come to her easily, but these pour from her eyes like summer rain. There's a month's worth backlogged behind her eyes— maybe years' worth. It's more tragedy than her body ever knew what to do with, and now it's got her by the throat.

Mary's arms hold her up like a storm drain, like Kathleen is only moments from being sucked down the gutter and into the depths of her own despair.

"It's good to cry," the tender woman says as Kathleen finds her breath again, somewhere between the soothing circles rubbed along her back. "We need to release. I cry all the time. For me, for Joseph, for you, for the world. We have to let go of the bad to make room for more good, you know?"

"I have nothing left." Kathleen gasps. "I have no one."

"That's not true," Mary whispers. She takes both of her hands, giving them a gentle squeeze before she presses them flat against Kathleen's belly. "You aren't alone at all. I'd say, you're the opposite of alone. You've got life in you."

Kathleen sniffles, itching to wipe the snot from her nose but not daring to move her hands from Mary's grasp. "What does that mean?"

Mary laughs. "Joseph always says I talk cryptic, but I think I'm just literal. I said what I meant—you've got life in you, Kathleen," she says with a wink. "Might want to stop by the pharmacy."

That's exactly what Kathleen does. Mary and Joseph promise to close up shop and hold onto the boxes until she has more permanent housing, and Kathleen leaves Jenkins' Jewelers for the very last time. It's not until the pregnancy test is purchased, swinging in a plastic bag at her side, that Kathleen realizes where her feet are carrying her next.

She could have taken it back to the hotel bathroom or even circled back to the shop. Instead, Kathleen finds herself at a familiar door, finger hovering over the doorbell.

The door opens before Kathleen can dredge up the nerve to press it.

"Aunt Katy," Haley says. "I've been waiting for you." She steps onto the porch, closing the door behind her. Kathleen can hardly recognize the girl. She stands several inches taller than she did a month ago, her tawny skin now a rich olive green. Her eyes have remained the same—big, brown, and beautiful. *Just like her mother's.*

"How did you know I…?"

"Uncle Michael told me you would be here."

She thought she'd run out of tears, but here they are again, stinging behind her eyes. "Michael? How?"

Haley looks to Kathleen's right, her eyes brightening to a vibrant green. Soon, she nods, turning back to Kathleen. "He wants you to know he's sorry. He's sorry he can't be here to help you with what's next."

It feels like she's swallowing a rock. "Is he here now?"

"He is."

Kathleen's sob rips straight from her soul. "Michael, I'm sorry. I'm so sorry. I can't believe what I've done. I miss you. Please come back to me."

A tear drips down Haley's cheek as she relays his message. "He forgives you. He says he could never blame you for what happened. He wants to know if you can forgive him?"

"Yes. Yes, yes, yes, I forgive you. I'm sorry, Michael. I love you."

Not a moment later, Haley's eyes lose their glow. "He's gone."

Distraught, Kathleen pulls Haley into her arms as if she could hold Michael through her. She knows better though, squeezing Diana's oldest daughter tight. "Thank you, Haley."

"I don't know what happened between you and Mom." The girl sniffles. "But I know she misses you. We all miss you so much."

"I miss you too," Kathleen whispers, and she means every word. Releasing Haley, she steps back to marvel at how much older the thirteen-year-old seems, beyond the inches she's grown. *I was around this age when I had to grow up too.*

"Do you want to come inside?" Haley asks.

"I don't know. Maybe for a little bit."

"Okay," she says, reaching for the knob. Before she turns it, she whispers, "Just so you know, Mom doesn't know that I talk to the dead. She, um, has a lot going on. So…"

Kathleen understands. "Your secret is safe with me, sweetie."

The door opens to the sound of music lilting from the record player.

"Mom, Aunt Kathleen is here."

The squeals of two little girls drown out the music in an instant as little Julia and littler Michaela bound toward the door. Julia clings to her waist as Michaela does her leg, and with gentle hands, Kathleen strokes both of their heads, marveling. *They're human.*

Julia lets go of her first, leaving Kathleen and Michaela on the welcome mat as she runs off to find her mother. "Haley, I think she's upstairs!"

"Go get her," Haley calls from the living room.

Kneeling to Michaela's height, Kathleen brushes the girl's caramel-colored hair out of her eyes. While her blonde hair has long since darkened over time, her eyes remain the same. *Michael's eyes.*

"Hi, sweetie."

"Hi, Aunt Katy." Michaela giggles, her gap-toothed smile utterly contagious. "I lost a tooth yesterday."

"I see that. Did it hurt?"

"Not really."

The stairs creak. Kathleen looks past Michaela to see her mother paused on the top step.

Diana's eyes hold a million and one apologies. Kathleen doesn't know what hers hold in return. She only offers a half-smile and lifts the pharmacy bag above Michaela's head.

"Can I use your bathroom?"

Diana smiles—still apprehensive. "You know where it is."

Dropping a kiss to Michaela's head, she stands, making her way toward the first-floor restroom. Diana's steps patter behind her, followed by Julia's.

"Can I get you anything?" her friend asks. "What do you need?"

Kathleen calls over her shoulder, "I'm okay."

"You sure?"

"Yep," she says, closing the bathroom door, the pregnancy test clutched against her heart. Meeting her own eyes in the mirror, Kathleen recognizes herself for the first time in… *Maybe for the first time ever.* "I just need to be with my family."